"W...   ...u made
you...   ...ng out into

...was shooting at you, Clay!" Her voice trembled with the knowledge. "You could have been killed. I—I couldn't stand it if anything happened to you."

Clay couldn't stand it. He couldn't stand to hear the sorrow in her tone. Couldn't stand to see her features crumple. He slid his hands over her shoulders and grasped her upper arms, resisting the urge to shake some sense into her.

Unable to help himself, Clay pulled Siobhan to him and fixed his mouth to her trembling one. Seeming shocked, she tried to pull away, but he held her fast, nudged her lips open, kissed her with all the passion of a man who'd never stopped loving her.

"What were you thinking? You made yourself a target by coming out into the open like that."

"It's your life I was worried about," she countered.

"Don't start that curse nonsense with me again!"

"Someone was shooting at you, Cash." Her voice trembled with fury and fear. "You could have been killed—bullets aren't afraid of a curse, Cash. They..."

PATRICIA ROSEMOOR

BRAZEN

TORONTO NEW YORK LONDON
AMSTERDAM PARIS SYDNEY HAMBURG
STOCKHOLM ATHENS TOKYO MILAN MADRID
PRAGUE WARSAW BUDAPEST AUCKLAND

As always, love to my critique group—Sherrill, Rosemary, Laurie and the birthday girls Cheryl and Jude.
Our birthday adventure in Santa Fe was a fun springboard for this story.

Recycling programs
for this product may
not exist in your area.

ISBN-13: 978-0-373-69528-7

BRAZEN

Copyright © 2011 by Patricia Pinianski

www.eHarlequin.com

Printed in U.S.A.

ABOUT THE AUTHOR

Patricia Rosemoor has always had a fascination with dangerous love. She loves bringing a mix of thrills and chills and romance to Harlequin Intrigue readers. She's won a Golden Heart from Romance Writers of America and Reviewers' Choice and Career Achievement Awards from *RT Book Reviews*. She teaches courses on writing popular fiction and suspense-thriller writing in the fiction writing department of Columbia College Chicago. Check out her website, www.PatriciaRosemoor.com. You can contact Patricia either via email at Patricia@PatriciaRosemoor.com, or through the publisher at Patricia Rosemoor, c/o Harlequin/Silhouette Books, 233 Broadway, New York, NY 10279.

Books by Patricia Rosemoor

CAST OF CHARACTERS

Siobhan McKenna Atkinson—Overwhelmed by her husband's accidental death, she's trying to keep the ranch from going under when the man she once loved walks back into her life.

Clay Salazar—Back in town to protect Siobhan, he suspects her husband's death was no accident.

Jeff Atkinson—The late owner of the Double JA was tracking a calf when he ran into something far more dangerous.

Raul Galvan—Why is the politician really wooing the dead man's sister?

Jacy Atkinson—Why was the dead man's sister left out of the will?

Early Farnum—What would the rancher do to expand his holdings?

Buck Hale—Is Clay's old nemesis trying to get revenge?

Paco Vargas—Why did the ex-con go to work for Buck?

June 22, 1919

Donal McKenna,
Ye might have found happiness with another woman,
but yer progeny will pay for this betrayal of me. I call on
my faerie blood and my powers as a witch to give yers
only sorrow in love, for should they act on their feelings,
they will put their loved ones in mortal danger.

So be it,
Sheelin O'Keefe

Prologue

Where the hell was that calf? Jeff Atkinson wondered as he stood in the saddle and looked around to no avail.

He'd tracked the sneaky beast for miles now. Third time the calf had gotten out of his pasture this month. Coming back from church, he'd ridden out for a quick check on the herd only to find the calf's mamma bawling at the downed fence, an area too small for her to bust through. Thankfully. Otherwise, he'd have more than a lone calf to worry about.

After following the calf's tracks along the dry creek bed lined with cottonwoods, he hit a sandstone formation where the tracks fell off.

Whistling sharply, he called out, "Hey, little doggie, where are you?" as if the calf would answer. Well, if he was scared enough, maybe he would cry to be found. No answer, though, so Jeff whistled again.

Exhausted, he wanted to get home to Siobhan and one of her special Sunday dinners. And to the weekly sharing of bodies afterward, a ritual for which he would never be too tired. He wished for more closeness in their marriage, but their situation had been doubly

complicated. He'd known she was in love with another
man, which hadn't bothered him at the time. After a year
and a half of marriage, he'd grown to care for her, but
unfortunately, she'd never fully switched her affections
to him in the way he would now like. They were, after
all, thinking of starting a family. He just had to take care
of a personal situation before they made that move.

Tempted to leave the calf be for now—in the morning, he could send out the boys after him—he knew that
was wishful thinking. The little beast could end up as
dinner for coyotes or a mountain lion. And he couldn't
afford to lose another valuable animal, not when he was
hanging on to the ranch with everything he had.

So he kneed his mount and pushed him up onto the
hilly sandstone formation. The gelding picked his way
carefully between rocks strewn everywhere.

Gradually, he became aware of sounds that had no
place on this ranch. Crashing…cursing…smashing…
like someone breaking up rock.

Frowning, he urged his mount faster toward the intruder. Who the hell was on his land? And what did he
think he was doing?

The foreign sounds got louder as he guided the gelding through the mouth of a small canyon. Once inside,
the first thing he saw was the calf lying on its side,
unmoving. The little beast's throat gaped where it had
been cut. It had bled out right there.

Raw anger curled in his gut, and not just because he'd
lost another animal. The calf had probably been bawling
with fear and had been killed to keep him quiet.

Ahead, a man was bent over, his face hidden by his

brimmed hat. He was throwing broken rock around as if he was searching for something.

Reaching for the rifle in the sheath at his saddle, Jeff stopped when he heard a metallic snick come from behind him.

"I wouldn't do that if I were you. You want to live… hands behind your head."

Heart hammering, recognizing the voice, he did as he was ordered.

Only something told him he wouldn't be going home to his Sunday dinner or to his wife's arms.

Something told him it was a good thing he'd gone to church early that morning, and before Mass had confessed all his sins.

Chapter One

"Don't want to get too close!" The scrawny kid with a coiled rope in his hand danced around the corral and kept his distance from the adrenaline-driven roan. "Looks like he wants to kick me!"

Clay Salazar grinned. Mankato "Manny" Flores was newly incarcerated in the New Mexican High Desert Correctional Center, even newer to the inmate horse training program. This was his first time facing down one of the wild mustangs rounded up from federal land by the Bureau of Land Management and meant to be adopted out. Man and horse had something in common. Having worked as a staff trainer for more than a year now, Clay had seen enough panicky horses to liken the animal's experience to that of a man being imprisoned for the first time.

"He does want to kick you, Manny."

"I'll show him who's boss!" The inmate waved the rope wildly and in response, the horse screeched and bucked as he ran off.

"Stop right there! You try to muscle a mustang and he'll show you who's boss." Clay eyed the frightened horse. "Stormcloud's not mean, just wants to beat you so he can be free again. I know you can identify with that feeling. Go ahead and talk to him, get him used to the sound of your voice. Wave that rope, but just to get him away from the wall and moving in the direction you want him to go. Show him you have no fear."

Which of course was wishful thinking, for if any inmate he'd worked with feared horses, it was Manny Flores. Why the kid had signed up for the program had baffled Clay until Manny admitted he knew he had to learn to do *something* so that when he got out he could change his life. Clay was all up for that. It hadn't been so long ago that he'd had to change his own life over a woman he couldn't have, and wild horses had given him that opportunity.

Unfortunately, Manny wasn't doing so well. The mustang hit the metal wall, fell to his knees and charged back up to his feet and straight for the kid, who ran like the demons of hell were after him. The roan circled, missing him, not stopping until he got to the opposite side of the corral.

When Manny smacked the rope coil against the wall and yelled, "He's never going to let me near him—this is my first horse—give me one that's easier!" Clay worried the kid's fear was progressing to anger.

Lots of inmates had anger issues, and the training staff's hope was that working with the mustangs would help the inmates learn some patience that would serve them well on the outside.

Clay said, "Calm down and back off for a minute."

Manny shook his head. "This horse is impossible."

"He's not. You just have to take your time with him and you'll win him over."

"You know so much, let's see you get in here and show me how."

Normally Clay would ignore the challenge, would keep his participation to backing up the inmate he was teaching to become a trainer. But this time Clay sensed he was about to lose Manny from the program, and that wasn't okay with him.

Like Clay, Manny was mestizo. Being part Anglo, part Hispanic and part Indian put a man at a disadvantage when it came to opportunity, even here in tricultural New Mexico. Some people expected you to turn out bad, and it was easy to meet their low expectations. What was hard was changing your life—he knew all about that firsthand.

The kid wanted to go straight and Clay was going to do everything he could to see that he didn't screw up his chance. So he climbed down from the fence and entered the corral. Manny immediately handed off the rope, scooted out the gate and climbed up on top of the rail to watch.

Concentrating on Stormcloud, Clay picked up on the horse's fear that had been exacerbated by the scared kid. He knew he could calm the wild horse if he could touch him. He had his Navajo grandfather to thank for knowing how.

After the woman he loved had married another man, he'd left town heartsick, had sought out his late mother's clan. His grandfather had taught him to use a soft voice and a gentle hand when working with horses, had inspired him to find a spiritual connection that engendered trust. The technique worked not only with horses, but also with people, too. Clay's learning that from both his grandfather and the wild horses had allowed him to become a better man.

He softly clucked at the mustang. "Hey, son, easy now."

Stormcloud snorted and stomped his feet before charging. Clay waited until the horse was almost on him and then turned his body and easily stepped out of the way. He next advanced on the horse, arm and coiled rope raised.

"C'mon, son, move along."

The horse bolted across the corral.

Clay advanced on Stormcloud again…and again… and again…never making a sharp or fast move.

Finally, the mustang tired of the game and stood his ground. He snorted and rolled his eyes at Clay with suspicion, but he didn't charge him.

"Good boy, Stormcloud," Clay murmured as he inched closer. "That's a good boy."

Clay locked gazes with the mustang and continued murmuring sweet nothings meant to mesmerize. It usually took a week for an inmate to get close enough to touch a horse being trained, but as his grandfather had said, Clay possessed Navajo magic. He'd learned to communicate without words, to soothe the wildness in a horse, to abate the fear in its eyes…

He held out the coiled rope and froze in place. Stormcloud hesitated then stretched his neck just far enough to nose the rope. Seconds later, he popped his head and snorted. Still he didn't skitter off. Clay switched hands, holding out the empty one, and continued making sounds meant to soothe. Hesitating even longer, the horse finally sniffed his hand.

A longing in the horse's gaze touched Clay and he grabbed on to it, wrapped it with unspoken reassurances, the promise of safety and comfort. He sensed the slight shift—a softening in the horse's attitude.

"I get it, son. Easy now," Clay whispered, daring to touch Stormcloud's nose. Continuing to mentally project promises that soothed the horse's fear.

The horse allowed the human contact for several seconds before shaking his head and backing away.

Clay grinned. "Good boy! Enough for today." Knowing that he needed to quit with the small victory, he backed off toward the gate to the chute, and about to open it, yelled to anyone in the corridor, "Back off, mustang coming through." He whistled sharply and waved the horse over. "C'mon, son."

Stormcloud loped past him and straight down the chute to the pasture entry where the rest of his herd awaited him. One of the other inmates swung open the gate and let him in.

When Manny jumped down from the rail, his expression was one of wonder. "How'd you do that?"

"With patience and softness, Manny. Things that would serve you well."

"Man, if I could learn that trick…"

"You can. If you want to, you'll do it."

Clay read the kid's gaze as easily as he read the mustang's. The crisis was past. Manny Flores was in for the count.

CLAY'S DAY WENT AS THEY all did. Busy. Satisfying. Lonely.

The job was his life.

He even bunked in a room on the correctional center property in one of the horse barns. This part of the facility was minimum security and wasn't fenced off, so it wasn't much like a prison at all. No need to get a house or even an apartment away from here. Other staffers went home to girlfriends or wives and kids. Wandering empty rooms would only remind Clay of what he couldn't have.

The woman he'd loved had sent him on his way with some excuse about a damn McKenna family curse.

Heading across the grounds for the mess hall at supper time, Clay knew the curse was on *him*. Just because he hadn't been able to have her, however, Clay hadn't been about to settle for another woman. Not that he hadn't tried more than a few to clear his mind and satisfy his natural urges. But none had stuck. He'd rather be alone than with a woman he didn't love.

Entering the main building through a back door available to staff only, Clay was making his way down a dimly lit corridor, heading for the mess hall, when he heard voices that made him stop and listen to the furtive conversation.

"The ranch's troubles aren't just bad luck."

"Trouble rarely is."

Clay recognized the self-satisfied voice. Incarcerated in minimum security or not, Paco Vargas was trouble with a capital *T*, though he always managed to skate around the rules without doing anything that would put him on notice. Or if he did cross the line, he managed not to get caught. Though he was in the inmate horse trainer program, Vargas seemed to have no real desire to change. Having had more than one go-round with the inmate, Clay could read him as easily as he could the horses. Hiding his true nature the best he could, Vargas was simply biding his time, making sure he looked good so he could get out and undoubtedly go back to his old life.

What was he up to now?

"I hear the ranch has been going down since the owner was killed," the second man said.

What ranch? Clay wondered, holding himself back from facing down the men and demanding an answer.

As if hearing the unspoken question, Vargas said, "I give the Double JA a couple months at best."

A prickle slid up Clay's spine. The Double JA was Siobhan's ranch—he'd heard about her husband's fatal accident several months ago. He lunged around the corner and faced the two men. Vargas was a little shorter than Clay, but he was muscular with a shaved head. By contrast, his companion Frank Dudley had a full beard and long graying hair that hung down his back in a braid.

"What's going on, Vargas? What do you know?"

The inmate put on an innocent expression. "The Double JA is like any other ranch in this economy, Salazar. Vulnerable. I just hear it's not doing so well, that's all."

"What interest would you have in knowing how well some ranch is doing?"

"Hey, I'm getting out tomorrow and need to find work. We was just talking about ranches that might be willing to hire an ex-con. Right, Frank?"

"Yeah, getting work. That's all."

Clay knew the men were lying through their teeth. It sounded to him like something was going on at the Double JA—more than a bad economy or bad luck, starting with Jeff Atkinson's death. Whatever it was, he would find out.

But as close as he'd gotten to some of the inmates in the program, no one was talking, he quickly learned. Because they didn't know anything or because they were afraid of Vargas?

Paco Vargas had a hold on the other inmates. A look from him would freeze a man in the middle of a story. It was as if he had some kind of mysterious power over them.

So, again, what was he up to?

Clay couldn't help but worry. He knew Siobhan was trying to run the ranch herself after her husband's death, that she was alone and vulnerable.

Was some kind of plot brewing against her?

Was Paco Vargas involved?

Though he'd tried to forget Siobhan, Clay couldn't just ignore a possible threat to the woman he'd once loved.

He knew he had to find out what was going on for himself.

WHY DID THESE TERRIBLE *things keep happening?* Siobhan McKenna thought as she hunkered down to check on her mare's injury. Garnet had been pastured for several days, and when Siobhan had gone to get her, she'd found the mare's leg had been slashed open and badly infected. Not that Siobhan had been able to figure out what had caused the injury. Luckily, she'd checked on Garnet in time. The vet had told her another day without treatment and she might have lost the mare.

As she changed the dressing, she thought about her late husband's fatal riding accident four months before and how she'd had nothing but bad luck since. Things kept going wrong on the ranch—costly accidents and mistakes depleting the ranch's resources—and the stress was getting to be too much for her to handle.

If only Jeff hadn't died...

A dose of guilt flushed through Siobhan. She'd believed Jeff was safe, exempt from Sheelin O'Keefe's prophecy, or she never would have agreed to marry him. His death was her fault—she knew that. If the century-old family ranch went bankrupt, that would be her fault, as well. His stepmother, who'd moved to Tucson to be with her widowed sister, depended on the money Siobhan sent her every month. And his sister, Jacy, who lived in one of the stone cottages on the property, had a small trust fund linked to the profits of the ranch, as well.

Finished with the dressing, she stood and rubbed Garnet in her sweet spots—nose, ears, chest. "Hey, my beautiful girl," she murmured. Garnet *was* beautiful, both in conformation and in color. She was a deep blood bay, her coat a shade darker than Siobhan's long hair, which waterfalled over her shoulder from a clip. "You'll soon be good as new, girl, I promise."

The mare snorted and pushed her nose against Siobhan's chest. Smiling, Siobhan pressed her forehead to the old mare's and inhaled her distinctive scent all mixed up with the odor of fresh hay. The mare snorted and Siobhan picked up on a memory—their first ride across Atkinson land together. She could "see" the canyon walls and rims laced with stands of juniper and big piñon pine trees. She could "feel" the wind whipping through the canyons, ruffling Garnet's mane.

Siobhan had always had this connection with horses. Communicating. Reading their emotions and memories. A McKenna gift, her mother had explained. Not that all McKennas had the horse connection. Not Mom, who raised and trained horses, nor her brother, Daire. Nor her cousin and best friend Aislinn. But apparently there were other McKennas with a similar gift. And others with very different psychic abilities.

The mare suddenly jerked upright and hit the side of Siobhan's head. Her chest tightened. Flipping around, her hair suddenly flying around her as the clip fell to the stable floor, she saw Jacy in the entry. Her sister-in-law reminded Siobhan of Jeff…reminded her of her guilt. Not that the siblings looked anything alike other than being tall—Jacy was pale-skinned and naturally blonde while Jeff had been ruddy complected and dark-haired.

"Looking for me?" Siobhan asked.

"Not me. Early. He stopped by to see you again. I told him you were busy tending to an injured horse. He tried insisting on coming to the barn to help you, but I got him to stay put. He'll get itchy feet fast, though."

Siobhan sighed as she stooped to retrieve the hair clip. Broken. She threw it in a waste bin. How would she put the good-humored neighboring rancher off yet again without hurting his feelings?

Reluctantly, she said, "Then I suppose I should go talk to him."

She gave Garnet a last pat, left the stall and latched the gate, then started for the house, Jacy at her side.

"Early doesn't really want you, you know," Jacy said, her long legs easily keeping her astride with the shorter Siobhan. "He wants the Double JA. No offense."

Used to Jacy's outspokenness, Siobhan said, "None taken."

Though she was pretty sure Early Farnum wanted both her and the property packaged together.

She spotted the rancher leaning against his big dark blue SUV. Not bad-looking, fit from hard work, Early was in his late forties, as his salt-and-pepper hair attested. Nearly double her age. Nearly old enough to be her father, something she'd never had. He owned the largest ranch in the area since he'd picked up a couple of neighboring properties in the past few years. The economy might be bad for most everyone else, but Early Farnum seemed to have deep pockets. There were rumors about a silent partner.

"I need to shower and change," Jacy said. "I'm going to town for an early dinner."

"A date? I didn't know you were seeing anyone."

"Raul Galvan."

"The state senator?"

"Don't sound so surprised. So you don't mind if I go shower, right?"

"Don't worry, I don't need protection," Siobhan said. Jacy rarely dated and Siobhan thought it was about time she found someone serious. "Early's harmless. Go."

Jacy ran off in the direction of her cottage, which lay out of sight of the main house. Siobhan headed for the man.

Early Farnum stood with the afternoon sun hammering down on him as if he owned it. Early's sense of entitlement was not his most attractive feature, and it kept Siobhan from being warmer to the man. She'd never been fooled about his intentions. He'd been attentive and overly concerned for her since Jeff's death, but from the first, she'd sensed his interest in the ranch was part of that entitlement issue. Maybe as was his interest in her. He'd asked her out on a date only once, however, for she'd quickly informed him that she was in mourning for her late husband.

So now he made various excuses to visit and take up her time, in hopes, she supposed, that with persistence, he would eventually win her over.

"Early, how are you?"

"Better now that you're here."

"I'm the antidote to something?" she joked.

"Loneliness," he said, then raised his hands before she could protest. "Now don't get ornery on me. I'm here to see you about the civic meeting in Soledad tomorrow night," he said of the closest town.

"I heard they were going to address uranium mining

in this area." An important issue, to be certain. She probably ought to be there.

Hearing another vehicle, she darted a look to the drive to see a black pickup truck on its way.

But Early's saying "I figure if you're going, you could use a ride to town" brought her attention back to him.

If only she could get out of it without just saying no. "Early, that's kind of you, but if I'm going into town, I'll want to run some other errands."

"I can wait for you, Siobhan. No trouble."

Hearing a door slam, she looked over Early's shoulder as a man alighted, the blazing sun in her eyes keeping her from seeing more than dark glasses, a black-brimmed hat and an athletic body encased in black jeans and a black T-shirt.

An errant breeze licked her and she shook off a sudden chill. Now what?

Surely no other bad news about the ranch.

Pulse fluttering, she turned back to Early, saying, "Look, I don't know how long I'll be."

"No problem. I'm in no hurry."

Siobhan simply didn't see a way out of it without being rude. "Then I guess it's a go."

"Great. I'll pick you up at seven-thirty sharp."

"Make it seven." She really did have some errands to run. Maybe she could manage it before the meeting.

Early grinned and backed off toward his vehicle. "More time to spend with you."

Siobhan managed a half smile as the rancher climbed in and started his engine. Only as the SUV slid away from her did she realize the stranger was standing just out of her line of sight. The hair on the back of her neck prickled as she turned to face him.

Suddenly her world shifted as she got an up-close and personal look at the man who was no stranger. He didn't remove the sunglasses, but he tipped his brimmed hat back on his head. Her stomach tightened as she took in what she could see of him. Broad cheekbones...rugged jawline...straight blade of a nose. Her breath shortened and she had trouble getting enough air. She couldn't see his eyes, though, not hidden as they were behind those dark lenses.

"Clay Salazar!" she gasped out, wishing she had something to hang on to so she could steady herself.

And then he said, "Hello, Siobhan." His deep, whiskey-laced voice still had the power to curl around her heart and through her insides.

Her gaze dropped to his mouth. To his oh-so-familiar lips now set in a hard, straight line. Totally unlike him, at least with her. That wasn't the only thing different. The connection she'd always sensed when she got close to Clay was missing.

Was it him, because he had changed? Or was it her? What if she touched him? Would she feel it then?

She couldn't think clearly.

Couldn't speak.

Couldn't breathe.

"Nothing to say to me?" he asked, his jaw as tight as his lips.

And even when her head went light and her knees suddenly felt as though they were made of rubber... still no connection. It made her want to reach out, flesh to flesh, to see if it was really gone—which would be good for her, she told herself. But she couldn't let what she was feeling show, couldn't let Clay think she needed him again.

So instead of giving him a warm greeting, instead of touching him as she itched to do, instead of doing any of the things her heart told her to do, she demanded, "Of all people…what the heck are *you* doing here?"

27

Chapter Two

Clay felt his spine straighten as he took in the woman who'd once held his heart in her hands. Same wide-spaced green eyes and full, wide mouth in a heart-shaped face surrounded by masses of fiery dark hair.

What wasn't the same was her closed-off expression, something she'd adopted that day nearly five years ago when she'd told him she couldn't be with him anymore.

"Nice greeting for an old friend, Siobhan."

As if with great effort, she straightened, too. He'd forgotten how tall she was. Her eyes were nearly level with his. No longer a coltish teenager, she was all woman, with a woman's full hips and thighs and breasts—voluptuous enough to fill a man's arms.

And his dreams.

Siobhan took a big breath and crossed her arms in front of her breasts as though protecting herself. Her color was high, her reddened cheeks and hair a vivid contrast to her turquoise shirt. "I didn't mean it to put you off."

Liar, he thought.

Why so defensive? Because he'd walked in on her arranging a date with a man old enough to be her father and her husband barely cold in the ground? Just thinking about it made him want to grab her by the shoulders and squeeze some sense into her, but he was determined not to so much as touch her lest the past return to burn him again.

"How did you mean it, then?"

"I was just surprised, is all." Her forehead furrowed. "So what are you doing here?"

What *was* he doing here? Looking at her made him forget everything but their past for a moment.

He remembered days…weeks…months of being happy, of having a reason to get up in the morning because he knew he would see her.

He remembered that happiness being jerked away from him in an instant when she'd sent him away because of some supposed family curse.

He remembered the darkness that had followed until he'd found a new path that had given him deeper understanding and control under the guidance of his grandfather.

Then he got hold of himself. How someone in this modern day and age could be superstitious was beyond him, but it was no longer his problem. None of this was—he was just being a good citizen.

"Is there someplace we can talk?"

"This is as good a place as any."

She was nervous around him. The slight tic at the corner of her right eye gave her away.

Clay scowled but didn't argue.

He eased into the subject. "So how many cow-calf units are you running?"

"This year? Nearly three hundred. And we have a dozen bulls and as many horses."

"Quite a spread."

Siobhan nodded and dropped her gaze. "Not that I can take credit for anything other than trying to maintain what Jeff put in motion."

Running a ranch this size was a big undertaking for someone with little on-the-job experience. She'd grown up on a horse ranch, not a cow-calf operation.

"Don't undersell yourself."

Her head whipped back up. "If memory serves, that was your problem, not mine."

Disliking the reminder, Clay scowled and took a deliberate step closer. Part of him wanting to take her in his arms—not that he would. "What else do you remember?"

Siobhan's mouth opened into a perfect bow. For a moment, she froze, seemingly unable to speak.

Then a slight intake of breath and she said, "Truthfully? I remember more than I want to." And again she asked, "Why are you here, Clay?"—this time with impatience lacing her tone.

Clay gritted his teeth. He'd come *for her,* but she was making it impossible for him to admit as much.

So instead he took on an official tone. "I'm on staff working with horses and inmates at High Desert Correctional Center—"

"I know."

He faltered for a second, then figured the word

probably spread like all other news did. Not much other than gossip to entertain people in the area.

"I caught a bit of a conversation between two inmates yesterday," he went on. "Something about the Double JA going down fast."

"Is that all?"

"Isn't it enough?" He stared at Siobhan. She didn't sound surprised and she wasn't denying it. Had her troubles already begun? "They tried to make it sound like casual conversation, but there's nothing casual about anything Paco Vargas contemplates. He's trouble, and if he's interested in your ranch, there's a purpose behind that interest."

"I'll keep that in mind. So why are you here, Clay?" she demanded.

"I thought you might want to know you're in danger." Was she being purposely dense…or was she trying to make him feel foolish so he would hightail it out of there? "It's my responsibility as a member of the High Desert Correctional Center staff to—"

"To warn people personally?"

"I don't know people," he said, forgetting his resolve and reaching out to lift a curl of her hair with one finger. "I know you."

Siobhan blinked. The skin between her brows furrowed and she slapped away his hand. "You think the ranch is in some kind of danger, then?"

"Paco Vargas is involved, so you bet." His hand burned where she'd smacked it, but that was not why he regretted his action. Despite his good sense, it made him want more.

"What can this Paco Vargas do when he's incarcerated?" Siobhan asked.

"Actually, he's being released today. He said when he got out he'd be looking for work on a ranch."

"Well, you've given me your warning, so thanks."

He couldn't believe she was being so casual with the information, as if she were simply anxious for him to leave. "What are you going to do about it?" he demanded, quickly invading her personal space.

She backed up a step and shrugged. "I won't hire him. Okay?"

"That's it?"

"What else do you expect me to do, Clay?" she asked, suddenly defiant with her hands on her hips. "Have a hissy fit or faint out of fear? Or do you want to see me turn tail and sell the place?" Her voice rose, her words sped up. "Well, I won't do either of those things. I have a responsibility to this ranch, to my late husband's legacy and his stepmother and sister who depend on the profits to live. I intend to keep this operation from going under no matter what gets thrown at me! If you have something else you want to share with me, something perhaps more specific about what you think might happen to the ranch or to me, then speak up."

Her sudden outburst shocked Clay into a moment of silence. So his warning came after the fact. He could tell she was *already* in trouble. Why else would she have such a defensive attitude?

"I don't have specifics, but my gut is rarely wrong."

"Again, I thank you for thinking of me," she said,

her voice calming, "but now I need to get back to work. You'll have to leave."

With that she spun on her boot heel and headed for the house.

And Clay stood watching her for a moment, unable to rip his gaze from her retreating figure, mesmerized by the fiery hair billowing down her back, the full jean-clad hips sashaying away from him. Seeing her so riled churned up memories that burned him through and through. She'd always been so certain of herself, even in high school where they'd met, so certain she could handle anything.

Anything but *them* and the McKenna legacy she so feared.

Clay stood there feeling impotent as he watched her open the door and disappear inside. He'd come to offer Siobhan help, but when push came to shove, he'd backed down. Again.

He wasn't done. Not this time. This time he wouldn't walk away as she demanded, not when his gut told him she was in big trouble.

He'd leave—for now—but he'd find out what had been going on at the Double JA.

Then he'd be back.

FROM THE SHELTER OF THE curtain in the front window, Siobhan watched Clay get into his truck and drive away. Her pulse was still racing and her chest was still tight. But was it because of Clay or because of his warning? Maybe both. Was Clay correct? Did someone have it in for her?

Was that why so many things had been going wrong on the ranch lately?

She felt oddly disconnected from the possibility.

Clay's sudden appearance had stirred up so many memories more dangerous than what had been happening around here. And yet he'd thought it important enough to face her, something he hadn't done since the day she'd married Jeff. Truthfully, she'd never expected to see Clay Salazar again. And now that she had, she was shaken inside, first because she was still attracted to him, second because the connection they'd once had—they'd *always* had—was gone.

Sitting on the edge of a sofa and closing her eyes, Siobhan remembered the day they'd met in the school hallway. Clay Salazar had been the new boy in town and school bully Buck Hale, surrounded by his all-Anglo gang, had backed Clay into a corner...

"I'M IN CHARGE HERE!" Buck said, sticking his face into the new boy's. His wild curly blond hair contrasted with his ugly expression. "This is my school, and what I say goes. You answer to me. Got it, mestizo?"

"The name's Clay Salazar and no one is the boss of me. Got it, gringo?"

Clay looked so fierce. And so vulnerable. Siobhan hated bullies. With a twin brother and mostly male cousins to fight growing up, she was as tough and fearless as any boy her age.

"Buck, are you saying you're my *boss?" she asked sweetly, getting in the middle of the confrontation. "Because I wouldn't like that. Not at all."*

"Oh, look, Salazar, a girl has to come to your rescue," Buck said, but he backed off and his friends jostled each other to get away from her.

Siobhan knew her power came from being a McKenna—no one would mess with her without having her brother and cousins down on their necks.

"I don't need rescuing!" Clay said.

But there was a wild look in his eyes that told her different. She didn't think he was scared or that he would back off if she didn't interfere. More like he was afraid of himself. Of what he would do if further provoked. Rather than putting her off, his hidden wildness fascinated her, made her heart race a little.

"Of course not," Siobhan agreed, curling her lips into a friendly smile. "But I wanted to welcome you to Soledad." She held out her hand for a shake and waited. "Siobhan McKenna." And waited.

Not one to give up easily, she could wait for him to give in all day.

Finally Clay reached out and took her hand. "Clay Salazar."

The walls and kids around them suddenly faded away, the sound of their voices and locker doors slamming became a distant echo. The only thing left in her world was this angry boy. Looking deep into his dark eyes, she lost herself for a moment. His emotion filled her, threatened to choke her. The flicker behind his eyes told her that he recognized her awareness, her determination to calm him down. Slowly, the anger faded and she surfaced from the depths. She didn't understand

*how it could be, but the experience was similar to her
connecting with her horses.*

Only it was different, too.

Scarier...

THEY'D BONDED IN THAT moment. She'd never connected psychically with another human being. Never
before. Never since then. Siobhan remembered everything about that first realization. She remembered everything about Clay. About them.

But the past was dead. Things had changed—the
connection was gone.

She'd changed him.

Another thing to stir her guilt.

Even so, he'd come to warn her, but why? Some sense
of obligation? The otherworldly link between them was
gone because of her. Because she'd rejected his love and
had married another man. She'd done it to save Clay,
but he hadn't gotten that. In doing so, she had slapped
away the connection even more brutally than she had
his hand.

Refocusing her thoughts on what was important—
the ranch—Siobhan made a sandwich to go. They were
moving cows to a fresh pasture in the morning, and she
wanted to check out the site, to make certain no ugly
surprises awaited them.

Hopefully, what Clay had overheard simply had been
prison gossip. Hopefully, he'd jumped to conclusions
and was worrying for nothing.

Why was he worrying about her anyway? After the
way she'd split with him, she wouldn't blame him if he

hated her. He hadn't understood that she'd done what she'd had to.

Armed with a sandwich and a soda in a small pack, Siobhan headed for the corral outside the barn where she'd left Warrior. When she got within a few yards of him, the smoky-black gelding nickered and sauntered over to the fence. She opened the gate and before she could reach for him, he snorted and pushed his nose into her chest. Closing her eyes, she pressed her forehead to his, thinking this was as close as she was going to get to Clay. She could see him now...

Coiled rope in hand, Clay moved in on the gelding with a soft voice and gentle hand...fear blossomed in the horse and then spent itself out, and Clay was able to touch him...

Warrior whinnied and bobbed his head, smacking hers, and Siobhan realized this wouldn't do. She clipped a lead to his halter and looped it over a pipe in the corral fence and got him ready to ride.

About to swing into the saddle, she hesitated when a fancy SUV drove onto ranch property. The driver pulled the vehicle up to the barn and got out.

Dressed in a well-tailored navy suit, his glossy blue-black hair styled in what was probably a hundred-dollar cut, the man looked out of place on the ranch. Though he was wearing sunglasses—designer—she immediately recognized the broad cheekbones and thin mustache over a full mouth—her sister-in-law's date.

"You must be Siobhan McKenna, owner of the Double JA," he said with a broad, white-toothed smile as he stopped before her. "Raul Galvan, state—"

"I know who you are, Senator."

"Raul."

"Jacy isn't here." She patted Warrior when he pushed her—he was anxious to go. "I mean, not at the barn or main house. She has a cottage up the road a bit."

"I know, but I wanted to meet you. I like to know my constituents, know how they think."

"About what?"

"Various issues."

"Like uranium mining?" Siobhan knew he was head of the committee that was pushing to open new uranium mines throughout the state.

"How do you feel about the mines?" he asked.

She soothed the anxious horse and swung up into the saddle. Looking down at Galvan, she said, "Maybe you should wait until after tomorrow's town meeting."

His handsome face immediately hardened into an unattractive frown. "I see."

"What do you see, Raul?" Jacy asked.

Siobhan glanced over Galvan's shoulder. Her sister-in-law must have seen her date pull up and had walked over from her cottage.

Jacy's little red dress and four-inch heels and a ton of makeup were a bit much for an early dinner. They gave her a commanding presence, though. As tall as Galvan and well-muscled from hard work, Jacy wore an outfit that pointed out her more feminine attributes. She must really want to impress the politician. And so she did, if Galvan's expression was any indication of his appreciation.

"I see that Siobhan here is staying up on the issues," Galvan explained.

Jacy pouted. "You promised no business tonight, Raul." She slid her hand possessively through his arm.

Leaving Siobhan staring. She'd never seen her sister-in-law quite so flirtatious before. Jacy must really have the hots for the man.

"A promise is a promise," Galvan admitted. He tipped his head toward Siobhan. "See you at the meeting, then."

Siobhan forced a smile. "I'll be there." And was relieved when Jacy dragged him off.

She knew how she felt about the issue—the money to be made wasn't worth the potential cost in human life—but her care was diluted by the fact that there were no mines in this area. Plus she didn't want to get into an argument with her sister-in-law's new man.

Getting her mind back on work, Siobhan headed Warrior for the high pasture. The ranch had to be her only concern now.

Chapter Three

Clay needed a drink, and where was he more likely to find out about any problems on the Double JA than in the only bar in Soledad? The Gecko Saloon hadn't changed much over the years. The bar was on the seedy side with a broken-tile floor, adobe walls that needed a fresh coat of whitewash, mismatched tables and chairs, and lights so low you could barely see the person opposite you. But maybe that was its draw, because the place certainly didn't lack for customers. Though it was still afternoon, a half-dozen tables were already occupied.

Behind the bar, the balding, paunchy owner spotted him immediately. "Well, if it ain't Clay Salazar! Long time no see!"

Clay shoved his hat back on his head and pocketed his sunglasses. "Tom."

"What can I get you?"

"Whatever you have on tap will do."

The owner/bartender pulled a beer mug off a shelf behind him. Filling it, he asked, "You been hiding out after that fight with Buck or what?"

Not wanting to think about the darkest moment of

his life—the incident that made him take a good look at himself and search for a better path—Clay said, "You're talking about ancient history."

"Seems to me that was less than two years ago."

"But in a past life altogether."

Sliding onto a bar stool as Tom set down the beer in front of him, Clay went for his wallet.

"Nah, the first one's on me. To celebrate seeing you again. So what have you been up to?"

"I started a new life away from here." Clay picked up his mug and saluted Tom. "Spent some time with my mother's people. My grandfather, mostly. Then I got hired to a job doing what I do best. I'm a government man, now."

The owner froze and gave him a fierce look. "You some kind of inspector?"

"Relax, Tom, I'm not here to shut you down. I work over at High Desert Correctional Center." He took a slug of beer, then added, "I teach inmates how to train horses."

Tom reined in his distrust and relaxed, elbows on the bar in front of Clay. "That is a change."

"For the better."

"So what are you doing back here? Wouldn't have anything to do with Siobhan McKenna, now, would it? You know she's a widow."

"I heard. Heard lots of other things, too. Like how the Double JA has been having some bad luck lately."

"What do you expect? Jeff ran that ranch, not her. I hear before he died she cooked for all the men, picked up supplies and ran errands. The only experience she had with animals was on her mama's place. What does a horse-crazy kid know about running a cow-calf operation?"

"I expect she's learning real quick."

"She better or she's going to lose that spread."

"And she's nearly twenty-six, a long way from being a kid." Clay nursed his beer a bit, then said, "So it's that bad on Siobhan's place, huh?"

"Maybe not so bad if only she would sell now, while it's still worth something. With the money she could get for the ranch, she could go anywhere, do anything. If she sells before it's too late, that is."

Clay had done his homework and knew how valuable the land was. Siobhan's spread was nestled in a valley in canyon country. Though it was rimmed with sandstone formations, a riverbed cut through the valley, so she had a continual source of water, and above the rimrock there was plenty of good grazing land, better than a lot of places in this state. The Double JA leased acreage from the state and bordered BLM land. The two extra tracts of land together more than doubled her grazing rights. A very tempting carrot for an unscrupulous potential buyer.

"So what kind of problems have been plaguing the Double JA?"

"Mechanical failures…downed fences…now a hurt horse. It all started before Jeff Atkinson had that accident on the property, though I hear Siobhan didn't know squat about it," Tom said. "The bank called in a loan that depleted the ranch's coffers."

"Any reason in particular for that happening?"

"Rumor is someone with influence had it in for Jeff."

Clay wondered if it could be that simple—someone wanting Jeff Atkinson to fail. More than likely, someone wanted the land. And how convenient that after the loan was called in, the owner happened to have a lethal accident.

If it was an accident.

If any of what had happened on the Double JA since was an accident. What had been Clay's seed of concern grew into a full-blown worry.

Tom shook his head. "Now that ranch is Siobhan's problem."

"How's her help?"

"Her boys are hard workers, but about a month ago she lost her cowboss. Apparently his green card was inherited and he was hauled off back to Mexico. Funny the way that happened at just the wrong time."

Clay didn't see anything funny about it. He didn't believe in coincidences. The more he heard, the more he was convinced someone had it in for the Double JA—or was lusting after the land—and wouldn't stop until Siobhan either sold the spread or went bankrupt.

Moreover, he was starting to think Jeff Atkinson's death was no accident. If that was so, Siobhan might be in more danger than he'd realized.

He asked, "Anyone interested in the Double JA land?"

"Early Farnum. His spread butts up against hers. He's bought up a couple other properties since the crash."

"No one else?"

"In this economy?"

If the spread went cheap enough—maybe a fire sale, with Siobhan desperate enough to avoid foreclosure so that she settled for a fraction of what the ranch was worth—someone could make a tidy profit on the open market, Clay knew. If not now, then in a couple of years.

But who would be low enough to drive a widow supporting two other women—one of them retired—out of her home and business?

Just then the door to the bar opened. Clay flashed a look over at the three familiar men making a bunch of noise entering, Buck Hale in the lead. Straggly blond curls poked out from under Buck's Stetson to contrast with a mean expression that seemed to have permanently settled on the man's face. When he saw Clay, his small eyes narrowed and his "boys"—Dave and Ricky, part of his old high school gang—snickered.

Clay felt the skin along his spine tighten, but he refused to let his reaction show.

"Uh-oh," Tom said. "You're not gonna start trouble again, are you, Clay?"

"I never *start* trouble. I just finish it."

"Oh, hell," Tom muttered, retreating to the other end of the bar.

"Hey, mestizo, what're you doing back in town?" Buck asked, sounding not at all surprised, as if he already knew Clay was there.

Not that Clay wanted to get involved with his former nemesis. He raised his mug to Buck and said, "I was just leaving," then swallowed the remains.

"Now that's not very friendly of you. Is it, boys?"

"Nope," Dave said.

Ricky poked his leader. "He's cuttin' ya, Buck."

"Is Ricky right? You cuttin' me?"

"To tell the truth, Buck," Clay said, setting down the beer mug and moving closer to the other man, "I don't think of you at all anymore."

"Maybe you oughta." Buck signaled his boys to leave them be and they sidled up to the bar. "We got an acquaintance in common, after all."

Clay didn't like the other man's smug smile. He had to force himself to remain cool as he stepped closer and asked, "Now what acquaintance would that be?"

"Name's Paco Vargas. He talked you up good, so I decided to hire him."

Imagining what the inmate might have said about him, Clay felt his gut clench. He'd known Vargas meant trouble for Siobhan, but he hadn't counted on him teaming up with someone like Buck Hale—double trouble for sure.

He slid right up to Buck and stared into his watery blue eyes. "Question is...how did Vargas get the job interview with him locked up in the correctional center and all? I don't remember seeing you around the place to check him out."

"He didn't need no interview." Buck grinned. "I hired him on the recommendation of a mutual friend of his and mine."

"Who is—"

"None of your business."

Clay had always thought Buck skirted the wrong side of the law, but there'd never been any proof. His hiring Vargas set off all kinds of warning bells, ones he couldn't ignore.

"So your daddy lets you hire the help now?" Clay asked.

"Daddy's got nothing to say about it no more. He's doing all his conversing with the worms. Buried him nearly a year ago. Hale Ranch is all mine now."

Buck's tone of satisfaction made Clay wonder just how his daddy had died. How badly had Buck wanted control of the family ranch? How badly did he want more?

"You aren't by any chance thinking of expanding your holdings?" Clay asked.

"You talkin' about Siobhan's spread? Now that's ripe for the picking. If I am thinking about expanding my holdings, ain't none of your business, now is it?"

At the direct mention of Siobhan, Clay had clenched his jaw tight. Now he worked it and drew on the calm Grandfather had taught him to seek.

Sounding far more civilized than he was feeling, Clay said, "Maybe I'm just trying to be friendly…you know, since we have that common acquaintance and all."

Buck laughed and slapped Clay in the shoulder. *Hard.* "I'm gonna tell Vargas you'll be missing him, then."

"Not so much."

"What do you mean by that?"

"I'm changing careers again," Clay said, letting his mouth run before he actually thought things through. "Coming back to Soledad."

"As what?"

"Cowboss. Siobhan McKenna needs someone with experience running her spread."

Buck's amusement faded to leave the ugly expression he typically wore. Giving him a wide-toothed grin—not that he knew how Siobhan was going to react to the plan—Clay smacked Buck in the shoulder, *hard,* and then left the bar.

SO EXHAUSTED THAT SHE could hardly stay in the saddle, Siobhan clucked to her mount and ran her hand through his mane. "We're almost home, Warrior."

Touching the gelding made her think about Clay again...

Not wanting to get bogged down in thoughts of the past, she shook away his image and instead thought about the long day she would have tomorrow.

She'd spent the last of daylight checking the upper-pasture fences to make sure nothing needed to be repaired. She and the boys needed to move cows to fresh grazing land, and it was warm enough to drive them up above the canyon rims. Rolling, native grassland populated with excellent forage—blue grama, buffalo-grass and western wheatgrass—made up nearly half the ranch.

If only she didn't have to oversee the trail ride herself...

Not that she minded running her herd. Siobhan simply felt drained by all the responsibility, all the unfortunate incidents one after the other on the ranch. She was quite simply overwhelmed.

So when she rode up to the barn and through the

dusk saw a black truck parked outside, she felt ready to cry. Clay Salazar had been on her mind since he'd been here earlier. He was too much for her to deal with right now.

What choice had he left her?

Dismounting, she called out, "Clay, where are you?"

A rustling in the barn followed by a low whinny caught her attention. Now what was he doing in there? After throwing Warrior's reins around a fence board, she decided to find out for herself.

"Clay, what are you doing in there?"

No answer.

She was too tired for this nonsense. Entering the near-dark barn, she threw the switch for light. Nothing happened. It wasn't a bulb—that switch controlled several lights. Now what? An electrical problem? Lord, she hoped Esai could fix it. The old cowhand seemed to know a little about all kinds of repairs. If he couldn't manage it, where would she get the money for an electrician?

"Clay!" she yelled, standing there for a moment, not wanting to stumble around in the dark.

But if Clay was within hearing distance, he wasn't answering.

Maybe she didn't have an electrical problem, after all. Maybe it was a breaker. Siobhan felt her way into the darker bowls of the barn, heading for the tack room where she hoped to find a flashlight so she could check out the box. She'd barely opened the door when the hair at the back of her neck stood straight.

Someone was behind her.

Even as she turned, whoever it was shoved her—
hard—so she fell into the tack room. She flipped to face
the opening as the door slammed shut, cutting off any
view of the attacker, cutting the last of the light.

"Hey!"

Now in total darkness, she flew to her feet and rushed
the door, but she couldn't budge it. Noises on the other
side told her that her attacker was doing something to
prevent her from getting out—she didn't have a padlock, but there were metal loops for one. She threw her
shoulder into the door.

"Ow!"

The wooden panel stood fast.

Furious, Siobhan banged her fists against the door
and yelled, "Let me out! Let me out of here!"

After several minutes of raising a ruckus, her throat
went dry so she stopped. What did Clay think he was
doing? Was this some kind of a game for him? Was he
trying to scare her so she would take his warning to
heart?

Exhaustion overcome by anger, Siobhan was determined to get out and give Clay Salazar a piece of her
mind.

She felt around the inky room, hands skipping over
the bridles and ropes, over the trunk filled with blankets
and hoods, not stopping until she found the shelves holding miscellaneous supplies. She slid her hand along the
shelf at chest level until her fingertips hit the flashlight.
It went flying. Though she tried for a save, it bounced off
her arm onto the floor. Several more minutes of wasted

time before she recovered the flashlight and switched it on.

Siobhan had never appreciated light more. Even this narrow beam had the power to calm her inside. She gazed around, trying to decide if she had anything that would knock down the damn door—it wasn't a real door but a slab of wood, an inch or so thick—then pulled back. If she destroyed it, someone would have to replace it. She ran the beam of light over the door itself. Because of its jury-rigged nature, the hinges were on the inside rather than in between door and jamb. Yes!

Back to the shelves where she had a toolbox. Finding a screwdriver, she marched back to the door.

"Clay Salazar!" she yelled at the top of her lungs. "This isn't funny!" She started working on the screws attaching the hinges to the wood. "I don't know what you're thinking!" She got them all loose, then started removing them. "If you're still out there, you'd better get while the going is good!"

With the final screw removed, the wooden panel swung in at her on an angle, still attached to the frame with a piece of wood jammed through the metal padlock loop.

Hearing bootfalls, Siobhan felt her adrenaline surge even higher. Righteous anger made her see red. She righted the panel and pulled it inside the tack room. And then she took the flashlight and shone it on the man heading straight for her.

She met Clay halfway and shoved at him, pushing him off balance. "What did you think you were doing?"

"What are you talking about? And why are you hitting me?"

"Locking me in the tack room—did you really think it was funny?"

"Siobhan, it wasn't me. I just got here, I swear. I heard you yelling, so I came as quickly as I could."

"Liar!" She shoved by Clay and headed for the barn door. "Then why is your truck parked right outside?"

Only when she got to the door, she stopped, dumbfounded. Though it was dark now, she could tell no truck was parked outside the barn. Warrior snorted and whinnied impatiently—she'd forgotten all about the horse. Mind roiling, she crossed to him now and freed him from the corral fence.

Warrior obviously knew Clay was there. Able to read Warrior as she had always connected with horses, Siobhan knew his fevered thoughts were of his trainer…

Clay gently bandaging a cut while murmuring something that kept the horse calm…making a connection just as she did…

Startled by Clay coming up behind her, Siobhan whirled on him. "Where is it? Where did you park your truck?"

Clay reached out and stroked Warrior's nose. "Hello, son," he said, his tone shifting into quiet mode for a moment. Warrior responded with a whinny and then snorted directly into Clay's chest.

"Clay! Your truck?"

"I left it over at the house. I was coming to see you, but you didn't answer, so I thought to check the barn."

The moon might not be full, but it provided enough light that Siobhan could see the truck just where he said he'd left it.

"You moved it," she said unconvincingly.

"I swear I didn't." Clay took the horse from her and led him to the barn. Warrior swung into him as though seeking the personal contact. "I just got back here a few minutes ago, Siobhan, I swear!"

Keeping up with him, Siobhan took a good look at Clay's expression—deeply worried. He wasn't lying. Once inside, he unhitched the saddle and lifted it from Warrior's back while she removed bridle and bit. She might not be able to sense *him* the way she used to, but she could sense that.

"Where's the breaker box?" Clay asked.

"Back there." She pointed past the tack room and handed him the flashlight. "You'll need this."

He disappeared into the dark.

Her pulse began to tick and she suddenly felt like throwing up. He'd warned her. She hadn't really believed him.

She did now. Pressing her forehead against Warrior's cheek, she focused inward, hoping to tap into the horse's memory. Undoubtedly he'd seen the truck's owner. But try as hard as she might, she couldn't get there. Warrior was charged up, but not by the night's disturbance.

The lights went on.

"The breaker didn't pop," Clay said. "It was deliberately turned off."

Stewing in silence, Siobhan walked Warrior past him through the barn to the other exit. There she let the horse out into the small back pasture as Clay retrieved the saddle and bridle and put them in the tack room.

"I need to check on something."

Clay grunted and she saw he was lifting the door back into place as she entered Garnet's stall. She assured herself the old mare was all right, then looked around the barn for anything amiss. Nothing. By the time she was done, Clay had finished reattaching the hinges and was swinging the tack door closed.

As calm as she was going to be considering what had just happened to her, she faced him. "If it wasn't you, Clay, then who?"

Chapter Four

"Paco Vargas." Siobhan paced the plank floors of her living room. He was saying a man she'd never met was undoubtedly responsible for locking her in the tack room. "What would some guy I don't know have against me?"

"Probably nothing, at least not against you. Now I'm another story, sorry to say. I read through him and Vargas knew it. We had a couple altercations at the correctional center, but he was forced to back down. He gave me the feeling that he wanted at me more than once. The door to the outside was the only thing holding him back."

"If he has nothing against me...then, I don't get it."

"He's hired help."

"Who hired him?"

"Buck Hale."

"Buck?" He'd hated Clay—and undoubtedly her, as well, just because she and Clay had once been inseparable. Enough reason to want to see her lose the ranch? "You think Buck wants to put me out of business?"

"I think he doesn't care what happens to you, Siobhan.

I think he wants your spread, and he's willing to do whatever he needs to so that he can get it."

Siobhan threw herself into a scarred leather chair opposite his. They were sitting before the stone fireplace. She'd put some logs on when they'd entered. Though it was late spring, as soon as the sun went down the air caught a chill, and she was already cold inside.

"Wow, two of them want this spread, then. The man who was here when you arrived—Early Farnum—he wants the place, too, but he's willing to put the moves on me to get it."

"So I noticed." Clay's voice tightened. "You know that and you're still dating him?"

"Dating? What gave you that idea?"

"You said you'd see him tomorrow night."

"He offered to drive me to a civic meeting in Soledad. That's all."

"You could have said no."

Why was he pushing this? And why did she feel as if she was backed into a corner? "What if I felt the need to be sociable?"

"Then you *want* to date him?"

"No!" And why did he care? "I'm newly widowed if you remember."

At the moment she had to remind herself that she was in mourning. Even if she and Clay no longer had the connection that had brought them so close, even if she never meant to do anything about it, she could still be attracted to his rugged dark looks that made him appear right at home in the rustic setting—stone house, plank floors, exposed vigas along the ceilings.

Realizing where her thoughts were leading her, she started. This had been her late husband's family home, after all.

She said, "I buried Jeff four months, one week and three days ago."

"You keep count." Then he asked, "How did your husband die, anyway?"

"A riding accident."

"I heard that part. But how exactly?"

"I wasn't there. Jacy and Tonio, the former cowboss, went out to look for Jeff. They found him dead. His neck was broken from the fall."

"Are you sure it was from the fall?"

"Of course. What else?"

"Did you ask the horse?"

She blinked at him and for a moment couldn't speak. Most people would think that was an odd question to ask anyone. Crazy, really. But not an odd question for her. Not for Clay to ask, either—he knew about her ability.

"I couldn't even if I thought there was reason to do so. They fell on a sandstone formation just below the rimrock. Why they were in that area, I have no idea, but the horse's leg was broken and Jacy had to shoot him."

Something Siobhan didn't think she would have been able to do. Her sister-in-law took everything that came her way in stride.

"So you only know that your husband's neck and the horse's leg were broken."

Her pulse suddenly shot up. "What are you implying?"

"That there could be more, things maybe Jacy didn't

notice. They probably weren't looking for proof of any kind."

"Proof?" She wasn't liking where he was going with this. "Of what?"

"Of murder, Siobhan. I think your husband may have been murdered."

Sucking in her breath, Siobhan stared at Clay. He was serious, convinced of what he'd said. A sick feeling filled her as she wondered if it could be true.

Could Jeff really have been murdered?

That would make his death no less her fault—she'd agreed to marry him and had passed on the curse—but if he *was* murdered, she wanted to know about it.

Wanted to see the murderer brought to justice.

"How do I prove it, Clay?" she asked, forcing herself to breathe. "If it *was* murder?"

"I'd say for starters, we go to the site and take a look. My grandfather taught me a lot in the short time I lived with him…but it's been four months since your husband's death, Siobhan. Four months of weather. Any proof may have been blown or washed away. There may be nothing left for us to see. We might not be able to prove anything. We may have to wait and see what happens next."

"We? What we? You have a job at the High Desert Correctional Center."

"I have the next few days off. And I have a couple weeks' vacation coming." He shrugged. "I have no other plans. I'd be glad to spend that time here."

"Let me understand this. You're willing to go

out of your way to help me get justice for the man I married?"

"I'm willing, and you do need someone, Siobhan. Not only to keep you safe but also to keep this place from going under. I heard you lost your cowboss. I'm available, at least on a temporary basis."

Siobhan's mind roiled. Clay here on the ranch, working with her. Unlike her, he had years of experience working on a cow-calf operation. Right after high school, he'd hired on with a spread, then had worked an even bigger one until she'd married Jeff. Then Clay had simply disappeared.

She couldn't fathom being so close to him again.

Couldn't fathom putting him in danger.

Still...

Clay had changed. Or perhaps they both had. Despite the attraction she still felt, she couldn't connect with him. Couldn't sense what he was thinking or feeling that had once been as natural to her as breathing. The psychic link between them had been broken.

That connection had been the reason she'd sent Clay away—it was the warning that most McKennas in her family had experienced, and most had ignored. But the connection was gone now, and she didn't intend to get involved with Clay anyway, which meant he would be safe from the McKenna legacy.

"All right," she finally said. "I do need a hand here...I can't allow this ranch to go under. If you're really willing, I can use your help just temporarily until I get this spread running smoothly."

She didn't want to take him away from a job he loved,

but if Clay had some time off as he said, she could use his help. And if he could somehow figure out whether Jeff was murdered, all the better.

"IT'S A DEAL, THEN." Clay was glad Siobhan didn't try to fight him on this—he would have had to find some way to support her whether or not she wanted it. "We can check out the site where your husband died in the morning."

She frowned. "It'll have to wait a while longer. I have cows to move first. It's warm enough to bring the herd to the upper pasture."

"When we're done with that, then." Clay got to his feet. "I assume you have room for me in the bunkhouse."

He'd have to go back to the correctional center to get his things. And to make arrangements to take his vacation time. Anything beyond that was a question mark right now. He would see how it went.

"I thought I would put you up at the camp," Siobhan said. "That way you'll have your privacy. It's about a mile from here, closer to the herd. Several horses are pastured out there. You can take your pick."

"What if I want to ride Warrior?"

Siobhan hesitated, and her expression told him she knew he'd trained the gelding.

Warrior had been his demo horse—the mustang he'd gentled when he'd first started in the program—his example of how it was done properly for the would-be inmate trainers. Warrior had been auctioned off several months later along with horses gentled and trained by the inmates.

How interesting that Siobhan had bought Warrior. Interesting...but a coincidence?

"If you prefer Warrior," she said, "of course he's yours. I'm grateful, so anything you need."

He asked, "Don't you ride any other horses?"

"Garnet, sometimes, but she's injured. One of those many accidents around here lately."

It didn't surprise him that she still had Garnet. Her mom had given Siobhan the mare for her birthday when she was a kid. Their bond was unbreakable.

"She's too old to be chasing a herd of cows up above the rimrock anyway," Clay said. "Stay on Warrior. Let me see what you have pastured at the camp."

Clay didn't like being that far from Siobhan, not after what had just happened to her, but he knew he didn't have a choice. Enough that she'd let him back into her life, even if as an employee, so that he could protect her.

No way would she let him into her home, though, not to stay. That would be expecting too much.

So when she started for the door, saying, "I'll drive out there—you can follow me," he followed.

Outside, he tuned in to the night, listened for any noises he couldn't place, sent his gaze roaming through the dark. Siobhan stood at her SUV, seeming tense until he nodded and went for his truck. They got into their vehicles simultaneously. A five-minute drive through the valley and into another canyon and they were at the camp.

Getting out of the car, he scanned the area as thoroughly as he had at the ranch house. He noted the stone camp house with what looked like a makeshift tack shed to one side…pipe corral backing it up…pasture beyond with horses peacefully grazing. Nothing amiss.

"C'mon, Clay."

Siobhan was already heading for the building. He pulled the overnight bag he'd packed from the truck and caught up to her at the front stoop, where a pile of cut wood was stacked to one side of the door.

"Wait. Let me go first."

"Be my guest. Light switch is to your left."

The camp house proved to be a large cabin with a single room that provided an all-purpose living area. A couple of scarred leather chairs like the ones at the big house faced a fireplace carved into the stone wall. Opposite, a counter with a sink, both a microwave and small coffee pot on top, and a half refrigerator below served as the kitchen and eating area, and a full-size bed along the far wall made up the bedroom. The place was empty of intruders. A single door on the opposite wall stood open. He crossed to what was a combination closet and bathroom with stone walls and floor. Also empty.

When he turned back to the room to signal Siobhan to enter, he saw she already had.

"You didn't wait for my all-clear."

"This is my place, Clay. I don't have to wait for anyone's permission. No one manages me. I can do what I want, when I want."

The same Siobhan, he thought. No one had ever been able to tell her what to do. Stubborn as she was, Siobhan would be opposite just so a person didn't get the idea that maybe she would follow orders.

Refusing to let her have the upper hand, he said, "I was thinking of you is all." He moved closer. "Your safety. This place is probably not the best choice for me."

"Why not? I thought you would like it better than the bunkhouse."

"It's just fine, but it puts some distance between you and me."

"Maybe that's the point," she said, sounding a tad apprehensive now. "I don't want you close enough to get any ideas."

"Ideas?" Unable to resist the challenge, he narrowed his gaze on her and stepped closer. "Like what?"

Siobhan gaped at him for a moment. And for a moment, he felt it…the internal probing. She was trying to link with his thoughts as she had earlier.

Again he wouldn't let her.

He'd learned enough from his grandfather as to how to hide his thoughts, which would keep her from making the connection. That connection that had always been between them was the reason she'd pushed him away once before.

"I don't want you to get any ideas about the past." She ripped herself away from him with what seemed like a great deal of effort. "We can't go back."

"No," he agreed. "We can't."

What he wanted, he suddenly realized, was to go forward. He didn't want to revisit a time that had torn him in two. He wanted to make a new playing field, give

Siobhan new challenges, ones he would never even have thought of back then. Not now, though. Later. There were other things that needed fixing first. Besides, he'd learned a lot about patience in the past year.

And stealth.

"If that's everything, I'll be going."

"Shouldn't we trade numbers?" He pulled his cell phone out of his T-shirt pocket and flipped it open. "What's yours?"

"I don't have one." She said it almost defiantly.

"You have something against new technology?"

"I had a cell. And cable. And the internet. Never had enough time for any of those things, but I had to pay the bills anyway. So I got rid of them."

Which told Clay how tight her money was, having to get rid of things people already thought of as necessities.

She said, "I can give you the number for the house phone."

"Go," Clay said, then tapped in the number as she gave it to him. Slipping the cell back into his T-shirt pocket, he said, "I'll see you at daybreak."

She started. "Six-thirty? Make it eight."

"We need to be moving cows by eight," he argued. "And I need to eat. I doubt the refrigerator here is stocked."

"Seven-thirty, then."

"Seven," he countered, waiting for her reaction. When all he got was a look from her, he grinned. "It's a date, then."

"Yeah, breakfast—you, me and the men." With that, she spun on her boot and left.

Clay sauntered to the window and watched her climb into her SUV and pull away. He waited only until she was out of view before leaving the cabin and opening the shed door. She wasn't the only one who couldn't be managed. She might put him out here, where she thought she was safe.

That didn't mean he had to stay put, not after someone already attacked her once tonight.

Especially not after he'd seen the gasoline can and rags stuffed outside the barn near the corral. He hadn't wanted to scare Siobhan, so he hadn't said anything about it. But he didn't believe in coincidences. The only question was...

Had her attacker intended to burn the barn with or without her in it?

For a moment, Clay felt as helpless to prevent a tragedy-in-progress as he had been when he was eighteen...

GUT CHURNING, FINDING it hard to just breathe, Clay slammed out of the crumbling adobe structure he shared with his mother a short ride out of town. Climbing on his motorcycle, he cranked the engine and shot off down County Road. Mama had passed out again as she did more and more often as she drank to make their lives seem better somehow.

Not that it ever did. Poor was poor no matter how hard they worked. His mother cleaned houses all day and he cleaned barns after school and on Saturdays.

Who knew what his father did?

Who knew who his father was?

Clay assumed his mother knew the man, but she'd always refused to talk about it.

Somehow they always squeaked by financially, but Mama wanted more for him—college, for one—and the fact that she couldn't provide that step up for her only son was killing her. He'd assured her that it was all right. That he would be fine with a high school degree. That he would be happy being a hand on a local ranch.

He lied, of course, to make Mama happy...only nothing ever did. Clay couldn't stop her from drinking, so he ran from her to put his fear that she was killing herself out of his mind.

Speeding along the highway, he felt his spirits lift as he reached the area where he was to meet Siobhan. This was their special place, the place they turned to when they wanted to be alone. Slowing, he slipped the motorcycle onto the mesa and kept moving across the rolling area until he got back to where oak brush attracted deer and elk.

Standing in a small stone shelter that had an incredible view of the canyons before them, Siobhan was already waiting. With her fiery hair whipping around her shoulders and a smile that could light a room, she looked so damn beautiful that he felt his chest squeeze tight.

Clay's heart thundered as he slid to a stop and launched himself off the bike and into her arms.

Siobhan laughed softly. "Such enthusiasm...and still you're late."

"It's Mama again." He shook his head.

She reached up and touched his face gently and inside his head he heard her say, It's going to be all right, Clay.

I know it is. When I'm with you, everything is all right.

No actual words passed aloud between them. They didn't have to speak. They could read each other, know what the other was thinking. He held her close, pressed to his aching heart, and once more savored the connection that he'd never experienced with anyone but her.

I love you, Clay. I always will…

Slowly, melting into her, he calmed inside. Siobhan was the only person who stood between him and the outside world. Him and trouble. Before her, he'd always been wild and reckless. But since that first day when she'd offered him her hand, something had drawn them together…something bigger than both of them. Rather than question it, he'd simply gone along for the ride. He'd never been sorry.

Loving Siobhan was scary sometimes, but mostly she was the salve to his often-bleeding soul.

She was his sanctuary…and his salvation…she was his forever.

He couldn't ever lose her or he would be well and truly lost…

His gut clenched as Clay forced himself back to the reality of the situation. He had lost her and he'd survived thanks to Grandfather.

Clay grabbed a bridle and stepped down toward the

corral, which was empty. Heading to the back pasture, he whistled softly, hypnotically. By the time he reached the fence, an inquisitive Appaloosa awaited him, and several other horses were picking their way across the pasture.

"Hey, son," Clay murmured to the gelding as he stepped through the fence rails. "You ready to ride?"

Locking gazes with the liquid dark eyes inspecting him, Clay projected calm. He stroked the Appaloosa's nose then ran his hand along his thick neck and back smoothly to make sure the horse accepted him. Flesh quivered at his touch, but the horse didn't move away.

"Good boy." He would do.

Clay stroked the horse's nose then raised the bridle, gently slipped the bit into his mouth and pulled the crown of the bridle into place up over his ears. Reins and mane bunched in one hand, he swung himself easily onto the horse's bare back and took off all in one motion.

Riding at night gave Clay a feel of the place that he wouldn't get by day. The dark spaces—the ones that could hide danger like a rock outcropping or a sudden dip away from the road—reached out to him. Thanks to Grandfather, he'd learned to fine-tune his senses, to hear what the average ear missed. The ability was different than what he and Siobhan had once shared, but it was equally powerful.

Tonight was quiet but for the horse beneath him as he rode hard to catch up to Siobhan.

Not that she would ever know it.

As they made a rise overlooking the main house, Clay

slowed. This was a good lookout point. Far enough that she would never know he was there, but close enough that he would be within shouting distance.

Hopefully it wouldn't come to that.

Guiding the horse into a bank of trees that would further protect them from observers, he hopped off and tossed the reins over a low branch.

Then he hunkered down, back against the trunk, where he would allow himself only a light sleep so that he could guard Siobhan until daybreak.

Chapter Five

Breakfast went smoothly with Esai and Ben keeping Clay involved as they ate large quantities of eggs and sausage and pancakes they got from the buffet she'd set out on a counter.

The kitchen might look rustic with pine cabinets and counters and plank floors, but she had every modern kitchen appliance a woman could want. Sitting around the kitchen table, her men detailed some of the incidents that had happened on the ranch in the past months. As she ate in near silence, Siobhan felt protected in their company.

"The worst thing," old Esai was saying, his thin, sun-leathered face drawn into a frown that increased the wrinkles, "was when we lost a cow and her calf nearly went crazy."

"You lost a cow how?" Clay asked.

The men exchanged significant looks, then young Ben said, "She got away from the herd." He swallowed hard and his soft brown eyes got all watery. "She was torn up, still alive but partly eaten when we found her.

Had to put her down. Never saw nothin' like that before. Seems coyotes got her."

"Seems?" Clay echoed.

"We ain't convinced is all," Esai grumbled.

Siobhan hadn't been convinced, either, but she'd had neither the time nor the money to prove otherwise. Someone could have set dogs on the cow and watched her being tortured for fun. She didn't want to think about what despicable human being would do that.

Despite the recounting of the ranch's woes, Esai and Ben made a good buffer between her and Clay. Maybe having him around wasn't going to be so difficult, after all.

Then Jacy showed up, waltzing through the back door dressed in tight jeans and a low-cut, short-sleeved T-shirt that showed off the muscular arms she was so proud of. Her blond hair was swept up in a ponytail, her face free of the makeup she'd worn the night before. Normally she ate breakfast in her own cottage, but apparently she was making an exception.

"Morning, Jacy," Siobhan said.

"I saw the truck sitting outside." Going for a plate at the buffet, Jacy gave Clay a hard look. "Don't I know you?"

"Could be."

"This is Clay Salazar," Siobhan said, thinking her sister-in-law must have graduated high school several years before Clay even moved to town with his mother. Undoubtedly Jacy had seen him around, though.

"Clay Salazar?" Jacy looked to Siobhan, her expression accusing. "*The* Clay Salazar?"

Siobhan flinched inside. Jeff must have told his sister about the man she'd once loved.

"Clay agreed to take over as cowboss for a time. With Tonio gone—"

"So you went looking for your old lover?" Jacy troweled eggs to her plate, seeming not to notice that a quantity missed. "Or did you know where he was all along?"

"Actually, I heard the ranch was in trouble," Clay said. "And that someone was helping it along. I was concerned, so I came to warn Siobhan. I offered to help her with the spread short-term."

"How convenient." Jacy tossed her plate onto the table then sat down and glared at Clay.

"Convenient that I had some time off," he agreed.

He certainly sounded calm, Siobhan thought.

"I wonder what my dead brother would say if he knew you were here, poaching his territory."

Clay was a whole lot calmer than Siobhan was suddenly feeling. "Jacy! You're out of line!"

"Am I?"

"You are," Clay agreed.

Though he didn't lose his cool, Siobhan noted how his gaze hardened on Jacy.

"So are you trying to pretend you didn't come back for Siobhan?"

Now all eyes were on *her,* Siobhan realized. She stood and took her plate. "Jacy, that's enough. Be grateful Clay is willing to help us in our time of need."

"Help *you.* The ranch belongs to *you.*"

Unable to argue with that, Siobhan took her dishes

and flatware to the kitchen sink. Esai and Ben quickly followed. They were clearly uncomfortable, as well. They scraped their plates and set them on the counter.

"We'll be getting to the horses," Esai said.

"How many should we tack up?" Ben asked in a low voice.

Siobhan glanced over to her sister-in-law. Jacy might be in a mood over Clay's appearance, but she never shirked her work on the ranch, and chances were she wouldn't now.

"Five. Saddle Chief for Clay. He's in the corral with Warrior."

"Will do," Ben mumbled, picking up his hat from the peg by the door and following the old man out the back way.

Siobhan stacked the dishwasher then started clearing the leftovers from the counter.

Jacy sat dead silent now, shoveling food in her mouth and glaring at Clay.

Clay in turn sat back in his chair and nursed his mug of coffee. Siobhan couldn't see his eyes, but she expected they were still hard on her sister-in-law.

They shouldn't be—he should give Jacy a break. She and Jeff had been as close as Siobhan had been with her twin brother, Daire. Jeff's death had nearly killed Jacy— just as Daire's would kill *her* if something happened to him. But Jeff's death had changed Jacy, made her more reclusive and moody. And obviously more accusatory.

More reason for Siobhan to feel guilty. Though she hadn't been *in love* with Jeff, she had cared for him, was filled with sorrow for his death, but her grief didn't compare to Jacy's. With her mother retired in Arizona, Jacy had lost her immediate connection to family. Siobhan had thought she might want to visit with her mother in Tucson after the funeral, but saying the ranch was the only thing she knew, Jacy had been determined to stay—she'd said work on the ranch was the only thing she had.

Truthfully, Siobhan had been relieved. Jacy did know the ranch—and far better than she. Jeff should have left the spread to his sister, not to her, but Jeff had his problems with his sister—problems he wouldn't talk about. Though he'd wanted her gone from the ranch, he'd never asked her to leave. Siobhan knew he'd hoped that someday Jacy would meet a man who would take her away to an easier life.

Maybe a man like Raul Galvan?

Thinking to ease the tension, she called out, "So how was your date last night, Jacy? Did it live up to that red dress you bought?"

"Raul is an interesting man. He'll do."

What an odd thing to say. *He'll do?* Do for what? Realizing her sister-in-law probably meant for sex, Siobhan flushed.

And looked to Clay.

Her pulse shot up and her heart began to slowly thump. Just the thought of sex brought her thoughts to him, made her wonder what it would be like. She'd never slept with Clay—that would have brought the curse down on his head for sure—but not because she hadn't wanted to.

"Ready to get started?" Clay asked, hauling the last of the dishes—his and Jacy's—to the sink.

"Any time you are."

Siobhan flushed again and quickly went to the door where she fetched her brimmed hat from its peg then rushed out and over to the barn. Esai and Ben were nearly finished saddling the horses.

Ten minutes later, they were on their way to move cows. Esai took the lead and Siobhan followed closely. As she rode, she kept her gaze roaming, searching for anything out of place. A glance back assured her that Clay was doing the same, keeping an eye out, watching for danger even as he learned the land.

Beneath her, Warrior was agitated. He, too, kept looking back at Clay. Not surprising since Clay had such a strong connection with the horse, a connection that kept making itself known to Siobhan.

She'd been aware that Clay had gentled the horse when she'd bought him. She'd gone to the Department of Corrections auction knowing Clay was a staff trainer—courtesy of town gossip. With her connection to horses, when she'd checked out Warrior, Siobhan had sensed the link to Clay. And when she'd bought Warrior and brought him home, Jeff had sensed it, too.

Her husband had never said anything, but the look he'd given her had told her she'd disappointed him again.

Though she'd tried her best to forget Clay and be happy in her new marriage to Jeff, Siobhan had never quite made the transition as she'd hoped.

And now she never would have the chance.

WHEN THEY REACHED the first valley pasture, Clay took over, assigning each of them positions behind the herd.

"Let's do this easylike," he instructed. "Keep moving in big arcs, keep your eyes on the cows like you're predators sizing up the herd. Don't make any sharp movements or loud sounds. I don't want the cows scared. I want them anxious, so they'll bunch together."

Cows that got too excited when driven would run wildly. That could cause stress and possible injuries to the animals, not to mention wear and tear on the fencing.

Clay kept his eyes on Siobhan, not just because he liked watching her, but because he was checking to see how well she was doing.

"Patience, Siobhan," he called out when she let Warrior dance around several cows off to one side. "Keep it easy. Big, slow sweeps."

To his satisfaction, she corrected immediately.

Within minutes, the cows and their calves began coming together. Cattle off to the sides of the pasture pulled in. Others hidden in brush rushed out, seeking the safety of the herd.

Once the cows in this pasture were loosely huddled together, Clay said, "Siobhan, Jacy—start applying pressure. Close in on them slowly, and when they start to move, fall back. Esai and Ben, keep your focus on any stragglers."

They functioned like a well-oiled team. Despite her lack of experience, Siobhan was learning fast and working the herd as hard as anyone else. Clay scouted ahead to check on two other pastures where cows were grazing.

When the others caught up to him, Clay asked the women to keep the cows they already had moving. He and the men dipped into the other two low pastures to flush out the rest of the herd. Eventually they combined all three into one.

The team kept at it most of the morning, pushing cows through a series of small canyons, each higher than the next. Finally they reached rimrock. The way to the top was a long path maybe ten feet wide.

"We'll need to split the herd again, take them up a couple dozen cows and calves at a time. Easy, so no one panics and hauls off over the edge. Esai, you go first."

The process slowed down, with each of them taking a turn, leaving the cattle to graze, and then coming back down to the herd for another go. By the time they were on the flat above rimrock, more than half the day was gone. Then they had to start over, interrupting the grazing cows so they could get them to cluster together. Next they would move the herd into one of the fenced pastures where they would spend the next few months.

The team was working smoothly now, and the cows seemed to know what was expected of them. But before they could move off, a commotion of thundering hoofbeats coming at them scattered the herd once more.

"What the hell!" Clay growled, looking to the west. Four men were riding hell-bent-for-leather toward them, two blue heelers running alongside the pack.

Siobhan pulled up next to Clay. "What does Buck Hale think he's doing?"

"Let's find out."

Buck was accompanied by his boys Ricky and Dave.

And by a fourth man. Clay knew it was Paco Vargas before he was close enough to really see the other man's face. He could tell from the way the ex-inmate sat in his saddle.

He and Siobhan rode out and cut off the men before they reached the herd.

"What are you doing on my land, scaring my cows?" Siobhan demanded.

"*Your* cows?" Buck's expression went all indignant. "I'm here looking for *mine*. A couple dozen went missing from my east pasture."

Clay got that Buck's east pasture must be butted up against one of Siobhan's. "What makes you think we have them?"

"My fences are all up," Siobhan countered, "so they didn't just wander onto my property."

"No, they went through a gate."

"How would you know that?" Clay asked, immediately suspicious. He wouldn't put it past Buck to salt the herd.

Buck ignored him as if he wasn't even there. He squared his angry expression on Siobhan. "We tracked 'em to your spread, straight to that gate. Now me and my boys are here to get 'em back."

"Are you accusing me of rustling your cattle, Buck?"

"If the boot fits…"

"Get off my land!" Siobhan ordered, her voice shrill. "All of you!"

"Not without my cows." Buck signaled his men, and the three riders headed for the herd. "They'll check for my brand." He turned to Clay. "That would be a reverse B married to an H."

"Let them look," Clay told Siobhan.

Her expression tense, she locked gazes with him as if she thought he was crazy to cooperate. Clay didn't back down. Finally, she must have remembered that she'd made him her cowboss and he was in charge. She nodded her agreement. He then signaled the others to stay put.

Buck's men shoved through the herd, scattering it. Great. They were going to have to gather the cows together all over again when Buck's men were through searching.

"Here's a couple!" Ricky said and whistled for the dogs. He gave them hand signals, and the dogs cut several cows and their calves out of the herd and pushed them back.

"I'll take a look," Siobhan said, cutting free from him and Buck.

Clay remained where he was, offering a silent challenge to his nemesis. Buck said nothing, simply watched as his men undid Clay's work.

Siobhan was in the midst of cows and dogs. She leaned sideways to check a brand, and Clay saw her body stiffen. She checked another and a third. When she straightened in the saddle, her shoulders were slumped in defeat.

"More here," Dave said from the other side of the herd.

Clay turned to see Buck's man cull them from the herd himself. He started driving them back, but Jacy got in his way and jumped down from her horse to inspect the brand. She went from cow to cow to cow and then kicked up a storm of dust in a fit of bad temper.

"So," Buck said, getting Clay's attention, "is this what Siobhan hired you to do, or was cutting into my herd and rustling cattle *your* idea, mestizo?"

"Or maybe it was yours," Clay countered, fighting the urge to slam a fist in the other man's face. Buck was looking real satisfied. Clay followed the direction of his gaze to find Vargas escorting several cows in their direction. "Maybe that's why you hired Vargas," he said, turning back to a scowling Buck.

"Think you can make a case with that? We'll see what Sheriff Tannen has to say about it."

"What's this about Sheriff Tannen?" Siobhan asked as she rejoined them.

"I thought I'd have me a heart-to-heart with the good sheriff," Buck said. "I know for a fact that he doesn't like rustlers, thinks they're low-down varmints."

Siobhan urged Warrior forward and got in Buck's face. "I'm no rustler, Buck. Lots of things have been going wrong on the Double JA lately, starting before Jeff died. Maybe his death was no accident. Maybe I ought to talk to Sheriff Tannen about that? Think he likes murderers, Buck?"

Even knowing her temper, Clay couldn't believe she was angry enough to reveal her suspicions. "That's enough, Siobhan!"

Whipping around in the saddle, she shot a furious expression at him. He imagined she had a lot she wanted to say to him, but she pressed her lips together in a hard, straight line.

"You've got your cows, Buck," Clay said. "Now leave and take your dogs with you." With that, he aimed a hard look at Vargas, who seemed amused at the encounter. "Especially that one."

Rather than taking exception, Vargas grinned at him. "Hey, Salazar, ain't you glad to see your old friend? You're not surprised, are you? Remember, I told you I was getting work on a ranch."

"Don't worry, I remember *everything* you said."

Vargas actually had the audacity to throw back his head and laugh at that.

"C'mon, boys," Buck said, turning his horse away from them. "Our work here is done."

He led them back the way they'd come. Vargas caught up to him and the men exchanged something that made them both laugh.

And put a burr under Clay's saddle.

"Do you think he'll really go to the sheriff?" Siobhan asked, sounding worried.

"Maybe. Especially if he seeded the herd to make trouble for you. He'll hedge his bets, make himself look innocent."

"What if he gets me arrested? I might not have enough money for bail."

Clay realized Siobhan looked scared. He'd seen her in a lot of moods, but never scared before. All his protective instincts rose, but he had to keep them in check. She wouldn't appreciate the personal touch.

"Don't worry, if you get put behind bars, one way or

another, I'll get you out. Let's finish the job here." He couldn't help the sharp note to his voice when he added, "So you're not late for your date tonight."

The scared expression immediately disappeared. "I told you it's not a date. It's a meeting." Spine straight, she rode off.

And Clay settled down inside. That was the Siobhan he knew...

The woman he'd never forgotten...

The one he'd come to realize he still loved.

Chapter Six

"I'm real glad we're doing this," Early Farnum said, glancing away from the two-lane road curving through the mountains to look at Siobhan.

She ignored the personal note in his tone and kept her gaze on the passing landscape—striated rock punctuated by stands of juniper and big piñon pine trees.

"Yes, whether or not new uranium mines are opened in this area is an important issue," Siobhan agreed. "We should be on top of the situation."

"I think you know that's not what I meant."

"But that's why I'm here with you, Early—because of the meeting."

"The meeting is simply a way for us to get to know each other better." Siobhan thought she knew Early well enough as it was. He held no personal interest for her. The only man occupying her thoughts was Clay...

That morning, he'd taken charge as though he was her partner in the business, not hired help. Or maybe something more. The way she'd caught him looking at her more than once had made her stomach knot with unresolved tension. He'd changed, all right. Since leaving

Soledad, Clay Salazar had matured into a real man, one who was sure of himself, one who set her nerves on edge.

She shook away his image.

Not wanting to be snide with Early, she simply said, "Yes, it's good to know your neighbors."

"Especially when they have so much in common."

He simply wasn't going to leave it alone, making Siobhan regret she hadn't been more direct with him. She should have refused the ride.

"Really? What is it you think we have in common?"

"Well, we have neighboring ranches in canyon country. We have the same concerns for our cattle. We're committed to our way of life."

"I inherited the Double JA. It's not something I sought out. It's not my dream life."

"Then why don't you put the ranch up for sale?" he asked.

"It's the source of income not only for me but also for Jeff's family. Plus, it's his sister's home—Jacy has always lived there."

She'd thought about signing the ranch over to Jacy—she'd seen the look of despair on her sister-in-law's face the day the will had been probated—but she knew there were reasons Jeff hadn't left the ranch to his sister, reasons he wouldn't talk about. Plus, she knew he wanted a different life for his sister. If Jacy owned the ranch, she would never leave.

Siobhan went on. "And Jeff's stepmother's retirement depends on the checks I send her. That would be horrible if Helen had to go out and find some kind of job at her age. All she knows is ranch work."

"But Jeff left the ranch to you—it's your decision, Siobhan," Early insisted. "You could invest the money and still provide incomes for all concerned. Then you could follow your own dream."

A thought that had tempted her more than a few times. But with the economy in the toilet and the ranch in shaky straits because of all the problems she'd been having, Siobhan didn't see how that was a viable option.

Not now, anyway.

She needed to get on better footing before making any kind of decision about her future.

But since he'd brought it up…

"Let's be honest, Early," she said. "My ranch is tiny compared to yours. So what is it about the Double JA that has you so interested?"

"Your spread is on quality pasture land with protection in the winter and plenty of water. You can run the same number of cows as I do on less land. And I have to admit I enjoy enlarging my little empire. My dream is someday to be the biggest cattleman in all of New Mexico."

"We don't seem to have much in common then, after all," Siobhan concluded.

That seemed to discourage Early. He quit the conversation and concentrated on his driving.

And Siobhan sank into an uneasy silence punctuated with more thoughts of Clay.

What was he doing now?

After they'd moved the herd, he'd ridden off to his cabin without so much as a "See you in the morning."

Surely she *would* see him in the morning—then they would go check out the site of Jeff's murder as Clay had suggested. The possibility that she might have put him off, that he might give up on her and not help her sort out what was going on, was the only reason she had to feel anxious.

Suddenly she realized where they were…within spitting distance of the place that she and Clay had called their own when wanting to be alone…

CURLED UP ON THE GRASS outside the shelter, Siobhan leaned into Clay, gathering his warmth, connecting at every level. Except that she was blocking some news he wouldn't take well. But she knew she had to talk to him about it, to tell him now before he heard from someone else. She had to give him fair warning before she had to leave.

Her stomach fluttered as she said, "There's a change in my plans, Clay." She knew he would hate this. "Next month I'm going away to school. To Colorado State."

Clay tightened his hold on her. "But you've already been in college for two whole years. Why make a change now? Why do you have to go away?"

The desperation in his voice nearly killed her. She couldn't look at him. Though she didn't want to leave him, she had to follow her dream before it was too late.

"The University of New Mexico doesn't offer what I

want to study," she said. "Colorado State has a great equine science program that I can't get here."

His hold tightened on her. "But CSU is at the other end of the world."

She'd fought her own wishes in the matter for two years because she hadn't wanted to leave Clay, but it was now or never. She'd always dreamed of working with horses like her mother did, but also on a more advanced level. She could be even more effective with the right education. Horses had always been her passion. Either she made the change in schools or she gave up the dream.

"It's only Fort Collins—less than five hundred miles," she said, turning in Clay's arms so she could look into his eyes. "I'll be home plenty. I promise."

"If you leave here, you'll forget me. You'll find someone else."

"I won't. I promise. I'll never forget you. And I'll be back sooner than you think."

His worry made her ache inside. He was in pain and she couldn't stand it. She kissed him and for a moment was suspended in time.

For a moment they were one…mind…heart…breath…

Not that she didn't want more, but she'd heard the stories, stories that scared her for him. McKenna stories. She didn't want Clay hurt because of her.

Maybe it was just as well that she'd be putting distance between them, at least for a while. It would give her time to think, to figure out a way around the legacy that cursed the McKennas into losing whomever they loved…

BLINKING BACK TO THE present, Siobhan realized they'd reached town limits. Recovering from the memory wasn't easy. She could still feel Clay's pain reverberating inside her. She steeled herself. She wasn't a kid anymore and she wasn't in love. A memory was just that...like a dream you once had but that you couldn't grasp.

This was the real world with responsibility to the land and to the people who depended on it. She needed to refocus her thinking.

The feed store was at this end of town, the community center at the other, the church and bar across from each other in the middle. Small shops and businesses, mostly flat-roofed adobe structures, surrounded them, all lined up along County Road. There was a small plaza, a square with trees and flowers and benches and even a little gazebo where members of the high school band sometimes played on nice summer nights. The grammar school was set back off the road to the east, the high school on a big piece to the west. Several dozen houses were set back on side streets, but the majority of people who would be at this meeting were ranchers, not townspeople.

Checking her watch, she said, "I just have enough time to stop at the feed store and put in an order. You can let me off and I'll catch up with you at the community center."

"You're the boss."

Siobhan figured Early was being ironic, but he didn't further challenge her, just did as she asked and let her off at the store.

"Catch you in a few."

"I'll be looking forward to that," he said, his expression gone sour.

Siobhan forced a smile and let herself out of the vehicle. Early drove off in a fit of dust, making her think maybe he finally got the message.

MAKING A MULTIPURPOSE TRIP to the correctional center, Clay arranged to take time off first thing. Other than a curious look, the coordinator of the horse training program didn't question him, just granted the three-week leave.

Would that be enough time to do what he needed to make sure Siobhan was safe and the ranch was running smoothly? His gut told him it was a gamble he was sure to lose. But three weeks was all he had unless he wanted to quit. Considering this was the first job that made him feel as if he could make a difference in someone's life, Clay wasn't ready to give it up unless he had good reason.

Unless he had Siobhan.

There it was…he couldn't deny it any longer.

He'd at first convinced himself he was only going to warn Siobhan that she was in danger. Then he'd thought he needed to help her because she had no one else. Now he knew that, no matter how hard he'd tried to convince himself he was over her, he still loved Siobhan McKenna, maybe more now than he had before she'd shut him out of her life. She'd grown into a fine woman with a sense of responsibility that went beyond what should be expected of her.

And she was still the woman who could make his insides twist with a mere smile.

He thought about her mother, Sorcha McKenna, who'd never married, had never seen fit to give her children their father's name. He'd always had the feeling that the independent woman had forced Siobhan to break up with him so Siobhan would be like her mother—without a man.

If that were true, perhaps he had a chance with her. Away from her mother's influence, perhaps she would see things differently. Only how would he know for sure? If he got too involved with her, Siobhan could turn on him again.

How could he ever trust her?

He was headed across the grounds to the barn and his living quarters to pack a bag when he heard the smack-smack of running footfalls behind him.

"Hey, Clay, you shoulda seen me today."

Clay turned to find a grinning Manny come up fast behind him. Setting his hat back on his head, he asked, "What the hell happened to put such a big smile on your mug?"

"I was able to touch Stormcloud like you showed me. I mean I really touched him, stroked his nose and his neck." Manny's grin widened. "His flesh didn't even quiver."

"Maybe Aaron was the right man to work with you," Clay said of the trainer who covered for him on his days off.

"Nah, no one is as good as you. You told me I could do it if I learned some patience...so I tried as hard as I could and it worked. I just wanted to thank you…you know…for not giving up on me. Anything I can do for you, tell me."

Clay's gut tightened with satisfaction. This made his job worthwhile—this kid turning his life around. "Just work hard and make me proud."

"That's it? I'll do anything for you, Clay. You just say the word."

About to tell Manny he'd already done it, Clay hesitated and thought about the offer for a moment. There *was* something the kid could do—be his ears and eyes here at the prison.

"I'll be gone on vacation for a few weeks, Manny. You could keep your ear to the ground and report back to me."

Manny's grin faded to be replaced by a more serious expression. His dark eyes snapped and he actually looked eager when he asked, "About what?"

"Paco Vargas may be making trouble for a friend of mine. The other day, I overheard him and Frank Dudley talking about it, and now Vargas is working for a man who doesn't like my friend much. Her ranch has had too many problems in a short time to just be a coincidence. That's why I'm taking time off—to help her and to figure out who's messing with her."

"Her? A woman!"

"Yes, a woman." Not that he intended to explain further, Clay thought, noting Manny's raised eyebrows. "I figure Dudley probably knows what's what, and he's got an itch to talk, so if you hear any more gossip about the

Double JA Ranch or about Siobhan McKenna, I would surely appreciate your passing it on to me."

His expression fervent, Manny nodded. "You got it. Any friend of yours is a friend of mine. I never liked Vargas myself."

Clay wrote his cell phone number on a piece of paper and handed it to the kid. "Ask Aaron to get you to a phone if you hear anything, but don't tell anyone else. You keep a low profile on this. I don't want anyone to target you in retaliation if I mess things up for Paco Vargas."

Manny stood taller and puffed out his chest, reminding Clay of the way he used to swagger around the grounds when he was first incarcerated. He'd lost most of that bravado since working in the horse training program, but obviously he could easily call it up at will.

"Hey, I can hold my own, Clay," Manny assured him. "Don't worry about me none."

But worrying was part of Clay's nature—he simply couldn't help it after the way his own life had gone south when he was the kid's age. "Just be careful."

After clapping Manny in the shoulder, Clay then started off for the barn.

"Hey, Clay," Manny called after him, "you're gonna be back, right? After your vacation with this woman?"

Feeling his gut tighten at the implication in Manny's voice, Clay turned to face him but kept walking backward. "That's the plan." Though he truthfully couldn't say for sure.

"Good. No one can handle a horse like you, and I want to learn from the best. When I get outta here, I want to make you proud."

"I'm already proud just knowing you want that for yourself," Clay returned.

Shoving aside the niggle of doubt that made him worry that maybe he shouldn't have involved the kid in Siobhan's business—or anything where Paco Vargas was concerned—Clay rushed to pack his bag.

Chapter Seven

By the time Siobhan placed her order and arrived at the Soledad Community Center, the meeting was already in progress, and Early was parked on the aisle halfway to the podium. He hadn't bothered to save her a seat.

"We have a different viewpoint on uranium mining than in the old days," Raul Galvan was saying, giving Jacy, who sat in the front row, a toothy smile.

The way Jacy was focused on the politician, Siobhan thought her sister-in-law seemed entranced. Siobhan hadn't even known Jacy had planned to attend the meeting—Jacy didn't usually care to involve herself in anything that didn't concern ranching. Apparently the draw for her sister-in-law wasn't in the topic, but in the man himself.

Siobhan slid into a seat in the back of the crowded room as one of the town council members said, "The courts approved uranium mining in northwestern New Mexico. If it comes to that, they'll do the same here."

"And endanger our drinking water the same as they're doing to the Navajos," a woman added.

A murmur set off across the room. People were

obviously worried about radiation poisoning. As well they should be, Siobhan thought.

Galvan held up his hands to quiet down the protest. "I've been told mining uranium only emits negligible airborne radiation."

Siobhan couldn't help herself. "Any radiation is too much risk, if you ask me."

The room rumbled with agreement.

"The state is going broke!" Galvan said, raising his voice to be heard. "The town is going broke. *We're* all going broke. Maybe uranium mining is the key to saving our way of life."

This time the murmurs shifted and some of the ranchers nearby appeared hopeful. Siobhan couldn't believe they were buying into this. Raul Galvan was a smooth talker, but surely they could see through him.

"Saving our way of life? That's a ludicrous statement if I ever heard one!" Siobhan lunged to her feet and looked around the crowd. "Uranium mining is sure to *change* the way of life you all say you love! It will destroy life as we know it."

"You don't know anything about it, Siobhan." Jacy stood, too. Her eyes flashed and her mouth tightened with emotion. "As usual, you want to run things your way. But Raul is the expert here and you have nothing to say about it. His committee has been studying the issue for two years. We should all trust him."

Early snorted. "I never met a politician you could trust. So what's in it for you, Galvan?"

Suddenly the tone of the meeting shifted again. Rather than discussing whether or not uranium mining in this part of the state was what people wanted, they began making suppositions about Raul Galvan's motives in sponsoring the movement.

"Probably going to get a kickback from the company he gets in here," one man grumbled.

"Or he thinks it'll do him politically," an elderly woman said. "Is that it, Galvan? Think this'll give you a boost up in your party?"

"Yeah," Early said, "he probably wants to run for the U.S. Senate so he can get out of here once he ruins this part of the state!"

So was Early against mining or not? Siobhan couldn't tell.

The only one who seemed to be apart from the discussion was Buck Hale, who stood to one side of the crowd, his shoulder hunched into the wall. He was watching and listening intently, but Siobhan couldn't tell which side he was on, either. He was alone—no Paco Vargas in sight—and keeping his thoughts to himself. It was as if he was watching the meeting on a screen like a movie, as if he weren't at all involved.

How odd.

And then Buck's attention shifted to her, and the small, smug smile he gave her sent a chill skittering straight down Siobhan's spine. What was he up to now? Making more plans to ruin her spread, to get her off the land?

"Calm down so we can discuss this rationally," Galvan pleaded with the crowd, drawing her attention away from Buck. "Let me give you the facts before you make up your minds."

But no one else seemed to be listening to him.

No one but Jacy. She moved to Galvan, slipped a hand through his arm and stood on tiptoe, her lips at his ear. Siobhan didn't know what her sister-in-law was saying exactly, but it was apparent she was trying to mollify the politician.

As if realizing the meeting was a lost cause now, Galvan rushed down the aisle toward the exit, slowing only long enough to glare at Siobhan. Long enough for Jacy to catch up to him.

"Let's go get a drink," she said.

Galvan didn't answer, simply gave Siobhan an even darker look—obviously blaming her for the ruin of his meeting—before sweeping out of the room with Jacy following at his heels.

The room began to clear. Siobhan glanced over to the wall, but Buck was already gone. She saw Early deep in conversation with one of his rancher cronies. It didn't look as if he was going to budge any time soon, so she decided to wait for him outside where she could get some fresh air.

She practically walked straight into Sheriff Tannen. A tall, wiry man, his longish hair white, his eyebrows and mustache still dark, he was nevertheless solid and immovable, despite his advancing years.

"Siobhan."

"Sheriff." She started to walk around him, but he put out an arm to stop her.

"You and me got to talk, missy. What's this about Buck Hale's cows on your property?"

So Buck had gone through with his threat. "I don't

know anything about it. I've been having enough trouble managing my own cows. What makes you think I have the time or energy to rustle his?"

"Now, I didn't say that."

"Then what makes you think I would know how they got on my land?"

"Educated guess?"

All right then. If he wanted her thoughts, she would share. "Maybe Buck put those cows there himself, then made a big show so that I would look bad."

"Show to whom? I understand it was only the two of you and some of your boys. So who was the show for?"

Siobhan hated admitting it, but Tannen made sense. If Buck had been behind the incident, he would have wanted independent witnesses so he could make a real case of it. Somehow she didn't see Buck as being innocent, though. It wasn't a far jump to think he was behind the myriad incidents on the Double JA.

"Are you going to arrest me?" she asked.

"Just wanted to give you fair warning."

"That Buck is going to cause trouble? Nothing new there. Why else would he have hired Paco Vargas straight out of prison?"

"Maybe he believes in giving a man a second chance?"

Siobhan gaped at the sheriff. Was he serious? Surely he was trying to put a good spin on the situation.

"Maybe instead of investigating me," she said, "you ought to be looking for my husband's murderer."

Tannen was taken aback. "Jeff died because he had an unfortunate accident."

"Or maybe it was just made to look that way," Siobhan countered. "Too many things have been going wrong at the ranch, too many to be just bad luck."

"What reason would someone have to kill Jeff?"

Aware that several people were turning to listen to the exchange between her and the sheriff, Siobhan said, "I don't know, but apparently you have no doubts about his death, so it looks like I'll be investigating myself."

Frustration seared Siobhan by the time she forced her way outside. The sheriff didn't believe her. Maybe no one would but the man who'd put the thought in her head in the first place. Now she couldn't forget it and worried that Clay had abandoned her and that she would be investigating alone.

And when she saw Early Farnum's SUV speed right by her without him so much as looking back, she realized she was going to have to get home alone, too.

Jacy had already disappeared. If her sister-in-law would even speak to her now.

Taking a deep breath, Siobhan looked around for a possible ride and realized Clay was around somewhere. That was his truck parked across from the community center. Relief released the bubble of pressure that had been building in her chest.

Had he come to find her?

Checking the crowd of dispersing people, she didn't see Clay, and he hadn't gone inside the community center or he would have passed her.

Where, then, had he gone?

THE FIRST THING CLAY HAD seen after parking his truck was Paco Vargas skittering around the doors to the community center. Vargas moved off into the dark but hadn't gone far before those doors burst open and Raul Galvan exited with Jacy Atkinson trying to stop him.

Galvan said something curt to her, and, giving him a furious expression, she stormed off.

Now what was that about?

Having meant to get to the meeting before it was over, Clay had realized he was already too late. His attention had been taken elsewhere, at any rate—on Galvan, who'd then gone after Vargas.

Now Clay didn't hesitate to go after them both.

What did a politician want with a criminal?

Was Galvan warning off Vargas or was he conspiring with him?

Their voices were raised in argument as they headed down the street toward the town's center, but Clay couldn't make out what they were saying. Skirting around vehicles, he tried to stay out of sight while moving in on them.

Then as they came in line with the church, noisy townspeople and ranchers flooded out of the community center, distracting Clay just for a moment. He quickly glanced back, searching the crowd for Siobhan. When he didn't immediately spot her, he turned back to where he'd last seen the two men.

Gone.

Damn! Breaking cover, Clay raced toward the church— a chunky adobe structure with rectangular belfries on each side of the building—and swept his gaze in every direction for Galvan or Vargas. Nothing!

The men had to be inside.

As he reached the walkway leading up to the heavy pine doors, Clay slowed. The church windows were dark and he assumed the doors were locked. He reached for the handle anyway and found he was mistaken. The panel creaked open.

Slipping inside, he stopped and let his eyes adjust to the dark. The only light came from a metal stand to the right of the pews. It held myriad lit votive candles in red glass holders beneath a statue of the Virgin Mary— offerings for favors for the people who lit them or as prayers for their dead relatives. He gravitated in that direction, and the sharp smoky scent curling off the candles assaulted his nose. Stopping again for a few seconds, he simply listened.

Silence surrounded Clay, but it didn't make him easy. No matter that the church seemed vacant, he didn't trust that he was alone. He sensed another presence. Vargas? This wasn't the ex-con's style—Vargas wasn't afraid of being direct. So why the game? Where was he and what were his intentions? Had he had a good reason for not wanting Clay to see him with Galvan?

Doing as Grandfather had taught him, Clay calmed his own breathing and wiped his mind free of extraneous thoughts and concentrated on the muted rustles of the dark space, on the barely audible creaks and groans and clicks coming from somewhere nearby. Or was it just the wind sweeping past the bells and down the belfries and into the church?

Was that whisper he heard behind him the wind or a voice?

He whipped around but if anyone was there, he couldn't place a body. He could, however, sense another presence.

Clay froze, waited for whomever it was to tire of the game, waited for the person to expel a sharp breath or to take that first step toward him. Vargas was trouble waiting to happen, and Clay was convinced the ex-con was having himself a good time playing a cat-and-mouse game.

Then a nearly imperceptible sound came from an unexpected direction. He whirled around on the balls of his feet, ready to lunge…straight into what felt like a wall of steel smashing into his head.

Clay crashed to the floor, his quickly fading gaze caught by the rapid flicker of red as dozens of lit votive candles flew toward him.

Chapter Eight

Certain the man she'd glimpsed going inside the church had been Clay, Siobhan raced to the entry. Instinct told her to hurry, and her instincts were seldom wrong.

"Clay?" she called as she swung open a door only to be assaulted by smoke. Eyes widening, she turned back and screamed, "Fire!" to the townspeople outside.

"Fire!" a man echoed. "There's a fire in the church! Someone call it in!"

Not willing to wait for backup lest it come too late, Siobhan was already inside. "Clay, where are you?"

A groan led her closer to the flames dancing along one of the pews. She could see something on the floor moving—Clay trying to raise himself. If he didn't move fast, he'd be burned! Covering her mouth with her arm so she wouldn't choke on the smoke, she ran to him, hooked her hands around his upper arm and pulled. More groaning was followed by Clay heaving himself up to his knees with her help. Coughing as he caught onto a pew back directly behind the fire, he struggled to his feet.

"Let's get you out of here before the flames spread!" Siobhan choked out.

The fire was gaining a life of its own, picking up bulk and speed, spreading along the pew and forward toward the altar. The church's interior began to glow red.

Siobhan tugged Clay away from the danger. He stumbled after her as several people burst into the church. A few were carrying buckets of water. Siobhan doubted they could put out the fire before the truck and volunteer firemen arrived.

She pulled Clay outside into the night, where he made rough gasping sounds that scared her. "Are you okay? Sit!" she ordered, indicating a bench on the church grounds.

He raised his hand and refused to move as he sucked in air. "Okay. I'm okay. Just need to breathe!"

"What happened?" she asked, trying to see his face by way of light from a streetlamp.

"Someone hit me." He put a hand to his head and winced.

"You could have a concussion!"

Siobhan grabbed Clay's face and stared into his eyes, dark pools glittering back at her. For a moment, time—and her pulse—seemed to stop. There were only the two of them as there had been so many times in the past. Clay was alive and she was grateful and without thinking she pressed her lips to his. Only when he responded, only when he pulled her hard against him and deepened the kiss so that her chest tightened and her stomach knotted with need, did she realize her mistake.

They weren't alone. And they didn't belong to each other anymore.

Gasping, she pushed him away. Embarrassment flooded her.

A growing crowd of people gathering outside the church had been witness to the kiss. A few people snickered. Feeling her face flood with color, Siobhan checked them over, searching faces for guilt.

Buck Hale stood at the forefront of the crowd, his expression dark. The other men had gone inside to put out the fire, but not Buck.

Because he was responsible?

"Will I live?" Clay suddenly asked.

"W-what?" Siobhan snapped her attention back to him.

"You were trying to resuscitate me, right?"

Siobhan clenched her jaw. "If you're *lucky.*" Then she relented. "You need to be checked out by a professional, Clay."

"Hey, no damage done. Well, maybe a headache."

Digging around in her pocket, she pulled out house keys. Attached to the ring was a small flashlight. Power occasionally went out on the ranch at the wrong time, so she'd learned to be prepared. Too bad she hadn't had her keys on her the day she'd gotten locked in the tack room.

"Sit!" she ordered, pushing him down on the bench and then flicking the beam in his face. "Both eyes are evenly dilated, but you're going to have a spectacular bruise by morning." A dark flush was already spreading across his left temple. Glancing back at the crowd—at

Buck Hale, who still stood there, unmoved—she asked
Clay, "Did you see who did this to you?"

Clay didn't answer immediately. He glanced over her
shoulder, and she knew he was staring at Buck.

And then he said, "Sheriff Tannen is on the case."

Sure enough, Tannen pushed through the crowd and
stopped before Clay.

"What in tarnation happened here? Why would someone want to burn down the church?"

"You'd have to ask the person who knocked me out,"
Clay said, his words half drowned by the wail of the fire
truck barreling down the street. "I went inside to have
a little time alone to think. Only I wasn't alone."

Though Siobhan knew Clay was lying about the time-
to-think part, she didn't contradict him.

"You didn't see anyone?" Tannen asked.

"Afraid not."

"Now why would someone want to knock you out
cold?"

"You're asking the wrong man, Sheriff."

The fire truck pulled up outside the church and the
crowd broke up, some people heading home, others
simply moving out of the way. It didn't take long for
the volunteers to get inside the church to extinguish
what was left of the fire.

When they were finished, a man trained as a paramedic checked Clay out. "You seem to be okay."

"I have a hard head." To Siobhan, Clay said, "I told
you I was all right."

"We don't know that just yet," the paramedic said.
"Symptoms don't always show up right away." He turned

to Siobhan. "You'll have to watch him for a concussion tonight. If he has a prolonged headache, dizziness, impaired balance or memory loss, get him to a doctor."

Siobhan nodded. "Okay, thanks."

Sheriff Tannen was busy talking to the volunteers, undoubtedly trying to figure out what happened. He'd donned latex gloves and was holding a big brass candlestick. Siobhan suspected the attacker had used it on Clay's head. Wincing in sympathy, she glanced Clay's way and realized he was looking a little shaky. She figured if Tannen wanted to talk to Clay again, he could ride out to the ranch or call for them to come in.

Siobhan faced Clay. "Give me your keys and I'll go get your truck."

"We'll go together," he countered. "Let's get out of here now."

Clay led the way down the street, away from the people still lingering around the church. When they got to his truck's tailgate, he removed the keys from his pocket and offered them to her without a fuss. Siobhan gave him a good look—to her relief, he seemed a bit stronger—and then climbed behind the wheel.

They were on the road before Clay said, "So, you're going to watch me tonight? Personally?"

Her stomach squirreled and she quickly said, "I'll ask Esai to do it."

"I'd rather have you…"

His suggestive tone made her pulse thrum and her lips vibrate. They were alone now, could be alone all night…and that kiss had stirred up old feelings. But this was no time to let down her guard.

Forcing her mind back to the situation, she asked, "What happened, Clay? What didn't you tell Sheriff Tannen?"

"What makes you think I know anything more?"

"Because I know *you*. Now spill."

For a moment, she didn't think he would. She glanced at him, caught a glimpse of his angry expression.

"I was following Galvan and Vargas," he finally admitted.

"They make an odd duo."

"Exactly what I thought. I arrived just as Galvan came out of the community center with Jacy. Vargas was outside and the next thing I knew the men were arguing about something. They went off down the street together without her. It was obvious Galvan said something to make her leave them."

Not very thoughtful of Galvan, Siobhan thought. Did Galvan really care for Jacy or was he just using her?

"So they went to the church?" she asked.

"I assumed so. I looked away for a moment and they were gone, so I went inside."

"Then one of them knocked you out? Vargas?"

"Sounds reasonable."

Siobhan's chest tightened. "Does he have reason enough to want to kill you?"

"I know he doesn't like me and I suspect there's not much he wouldn't do for money, but I'm not sure that's it."

"I don't get it."

"What if it's as simple as one of them spotted me and

didn't want to be seen together? A state senator and an ex-con..."

"You're thinking it could have been Galvan? Vargas would have no reason to cover, but a politician being seen with an ex-con might."

"No rush to judgment here because I didn't see who-ever it was who knocked me out. But maybe."

They both sank into silence. Siobhan couldn't stop her mind from wandering, worrying, couldn't stop herself from speculating. Back for two days—forty-eight hours working for her—and already Clay was in danger.

A chill seeped through her to her very bones.

When she drove onto ranch property, Clay said, "You're not really going to pull Esai from whatever he's doing to babysit me, are you?"

"He wouldn't mind."

"You're afraid to be alone with me."

Maybe she was, but that wasn't uppermost on her mind. "I'm just thinking this is all wrong, Clay. I'm the reason you got hurt tonight."

The McKenna Legacy at work?

That couldn't be, though. The connection was gone, she reminded herself.

"You weren't even there," Clay said. "Look, this prob-ably has nothing to do with you at all. Undoubtedly it *was* Paco Vargas. He couldn't get around me when he did his time. A man like Vargas wants to be in charge, which meant we had a couple of altercations at the cor-rectional center. He's probably been waiting for an op-portunity to get even."

"To *kill* you?"

"If he had wanted me dead I would be dead," Clay said flatly. "I think he threw over the votive stand to buy time to get out of there."

"But you could have burned to death," she argued, suddenly remembering Buck Hale had been there for the show.

"But I didn't."

What if it hadn't been Vargas at all? After what had happened between them, Buck might want to see Clay dead.

"Thankfully, I got there in time," she muttered.

"My heroine."

Clay was being dismissive of the danger again. Siobhan wanted to argue, to convince him to take the possibility seriously. Considering he thought Jeff had been murdered, she couldn't believe he was being so cavalier with his own life.

Having arrived at the split in the road, she had to decide whether or not she was going to take Clay over to the bunkhouse and ask Esai to keep watch over him tonight. Getting too close to Clay was unwise—she couldn't forget how easily she'd slipped and kissed him out of relief that he was all right—and yet she wasn't done with him just yet.

Truthfully, she feared to let him out of her sight, so she headed for the house.

Parking near the door, Siobhan waited until they were inside before asking, "So why didn't you tell Sheriff Tannen what you just told me?"

"Because I don't have proof, Siobhan. It would go

nowhere. And in the meantime, I don't need Vargas warned that I'm onto him. Or Galvan."

"Or Buck Hale. He was one of the first to get to the church after I sounded the alert."

"So he didn't do anything to help, not even to put out the fire. Well, if you can't depend on anything else about Buck, he always stays true to his nature."

Now that the crisis had passed, Siobhan felt let down. And more than a little apprehensive. Clay seemed himself…and that was the problem.

SIOBHAN WAS A BUNDLE OF nerves. Clay didn't have to rely on any psychic connection to be aware of that. He only wondered which bothered her more—the dangerous situation at the church or the one right here in her home.

He couldn't help himself. "So where do I sleep tonight? The couch? Or…?"

"Or?"

"I thought you might have something else in mind."

"I—I don't have an extra bedroom. It was made into an office."

He didn't say anything, simply kept staring at her. Her fair skin flushed and he felt his belly heat in response.

"The couch," she said. "I'll get blankets and pillows. Anything else you want? Chili? Tea?"

"You."

Siobhan blinked and licked her lips, and Clay appreciated how apprehensive he made her. Not that he thought anything was going to happen between them. Or that anything should. He just couldn't help himself.

He couldn't help remembering another time of crisis…

"SORRY, KID." Sheriff Tannen pulled down the sheet so Clay could identify the body.

Clay's eyes filled but he didn't let the tears go. With her graying hair loose around her narrow face, Mama looked so small and helpless on that slab. She looked as if she was sleeping, as though she might wake up any minute…

Only he knew she would never wake up again.

"What happened?" he choked out.

"She drowned in the creek," the sheriff told him. "The one right outside of town."

"How?"

"An accident. It was an accident, son. She'd been drinking, said she was going to walk home. It was raining, slippery. She must have lost her footing. It was an accident, Clay…a terrible accident…"

Clay nodded as if he understood when his center was molten, threatening to erupt. The pressure had been building since he'd gotten up that morning and realized Mama had never come home. How was he supposed to understand losing the only family he had? How was he supposed to get along now with Siobhan away at school and Mama gone?

"Is there somebody I can call for you?" Tannen asked.

"No one," Clay returned.

He'd never met any of Mama's family. He'd never been west of Albuquerque. He'd never been anywhere. He was an adult now. Twenty-one. A man with a job and a heap of responsibility. So why did he suddenly feel like a lost kid?

"What about Siobhan?" Tannen asked, his voice kind. "I know she's your girl. You want me to call her for you?"

Clay shook his head and backed off. "You won't get her...she's not here...she's five hundred miles from here in Fort Collins..."

And despite her promises, she hadn't been home once during the year. He hadn't seen her since last summer.

He flew out of the clinic and threw himself on his motorcycle and beat the hell out of town. He rode fast and hard and recklessly...the way he'd learned to live since Siobhan had left. And when he burned all his gas, he abandoned the cycle at the side of the road and ran on foot. He didn't know for how long—hours—until it grew dark. Eventually, he found himself at the shelter. At his and Siobhan's place.

He dropped to his knees on the ground.

He had nothing left. No breath. No stamina. No hope.

He was done. Spent.

Alone.

He must have slept. He didn't know how long. Dawn was breaking when a noise pulled him up out of a deep, cottony world. He stirred. Sat. Started when he realized that a vehicle was pulling up. Started but didn't move.

A car door slammed and then he heard her voice.

"Clay, Sheriff Tannen called me to tell me about your mother! I came as fast as I could!"

Siobhan flew at him and he caught her and held her tight. She'd come back for him! She'd come to share in his grief. She did love him, after all.

At last the tears fell.

Siobhan was all he had left in the world that mattered now and he would never let her go...

CLAY BLINKED AND HE WAS back in the room with her. A room that suddenly felt too close.

He hadn't let her go. She'd shoved him away. He had to remember that. Had to remember that he couldn't trust her, not when it came to them.

"I should go over to the bunkhouse. You need a good night's sleep."

"No, it's not a problem. You can have my bed. I'll sleep on the couch," she offered.

"It's not the bed, Siobhan."

Heading for the door, he didn't finish his thought: *It's you.*

Chapter Nine

"Ready to head out?" Siobhan asked, voice tight, as she stacked the dishwasher the next morning.

Clay figured she was uncomfortable with him because of the kiss she now undoubtedly regretted. They were alone in the house. Esai and Ben were already on the job. Clay was certain the tension between him and Siobhan had inspired the men to inhale their breakfasts and run. Undoubtedly, they already had the horses saddled and waiting for them.

"I just need to make a couple of calls about Galvan while I can get a signal."

Pulling out his cell phone, Clay clicked on the number for the trainer office at the correctional center.

What if they did find something that proved Siobhan's late husband had been murdered?

No doubt that would send her in a tailspin. Not wanting to think about that part—about her emotional commitment to another man—Clay concentrated on the fact that he was doing this to protect Siobhan. As long as the murderer roamed free, she never would be safe.

"Trainer's office," came a familiar voice at the other end of the phone.

"Aaron, it's Clay. Is Manny around? I need to talk to him for just a minute."

"I just saw him. Hang on."

As he waited, Clay watched Siobhan straighten the kitchen. She was self-conscious this morning, darting her gaze away from him whenever she realized he was looking at her. Still thinking about what might have happened if he'd bunked in the house as she'd wanted? The thought had buzzed around in his head all night, both when he'd been awake and asleep. He couldn't get it out of his head now, even though he knew it was a bad idea.

"Hey, Clay?" Manny said, lowering his voice to a near whisper. "Sorry, but I don't got nothin' for you yet."

"That's okay. I have something else in mind. I'm trying to get some information on Raul Galvan."

"The politician?"

"Then you know who he is."

"Everyone knows." Manny kept his voice low. It sounded muffled, as if he was covering his mouth with his free hand. "He's the one who's big on bringing uranium mining to this part of the state."

"Keep listening, and if you get the opportunity, maybe you can find a way to bring up Galvan's name. There's an article about his spearheading the push to mine uranium in today's *Albuquerque Journal*."

Clay had skimmed the article over breakfast. Unfortunately, it hadn't given him anything new.

"I'll get hold of one in the mess hall. I can say something about it, see what happens."

"That's the idea. If something is up between Galvan and Vargas, chances are Frank Dudley knows about it. Just be careful it doesn't look like you're *too* interested."

"Got it."

"Thanks, Manny. If you learn anything, go only to Aaron to make the call. Tell him I told you to call me."

He didn't want the kid to take any chances. He knew he could trust the other staff trainer.

When he hung up, Siobhan was focused on him. His pulse sped up and he waited for her to say whatever was on her mind. Her forehead furrowed and she turned toward the door where she spent an inordinate amount of time poking at her hair and putting on her hat.

"One more call," Clay said, hitting his speed dial.

John Whitehorse, a Navajo political science teacher he'd met while living with Grandfather, sounded happy to hear from him.

"Listen, John, I thought with the uranium mining issue affecting the Navajo Nation, you might know something about Raul Galvan."

"The blood-sucking politician? Hit me."

"I'm back in Soledad where he had a meeting about bringing mining to this area last night. The meeting didn't go well. I'm wondering about his angle at spending so much time here. He's wooing the sister-in-law of a friend."

"Tell her to run."

"That bad?"

"Worse. I've heard rumors of his being in the pocket of the mining company trying to break into that area. Nothing specific."

"Do you think you could get me more?"

"With pleasure, my friend. How soon do you need the information?"

"How soon can you get it?"

Hopefully both Manny and John would get something that would enlighten them about Galvan's motivations. Ready to ride, he joined Siobhan at the door.

"I'm glad you're asking around," she said, "but I can't help wonder what you think Raul Galvan had against Jeff or this ranch. And how he would have managed to make so many things go wrong."

"I wouldn't know. You tell me."

She shook her head. "If Jeff even knew him, he never mentioned it."

"How did your sister-in-law meet him anyway?"

Siobhan shrugged. "I'll have to ask her when she shows up."

Clay had been surprised that Jacy hadn't appeared for breakfast. He'd wondered where she'd gotten herself off to—though she hadn't seemed happy with Galvan the night before, she might have allowed herself to be wooed back and into his bed. She could be with him now. Not that he was going to bring up the subject. He didn't need to think about beds or what went on in them. He needed to keep his mind where it belonged.

He needed to do whatever it took to protect Siobhan.

A HALF-HOUR RIDE TOOK them to the area where Jacy and Tonio had found Jeff and his horse after the accident. Siobhan showed him exactly where they'd found the bodies, then steeled herself as they dismounted.

Clay gazed around without moving.

There was something weird about his silent assessment…an absence of sorts…as if he wasn't really there mentally.

The thought shot a chill down her spine.

Wanting to know what Clay was up to, Siobhan again tried to connect to him, again hit a wall and gave up in frustration. No matter how much she wanted to know what he was thinking, she wouldn't ask. He was too damned focused to even know she was there.

Finally he moved, picked his way up the rock, hunkered down on his haunches and swept his gaze across the ground.

More chills.

Siobhan concentrated on the area now to see if she could pick up on whatever was bothering him.

The wind soughed as it fluttered around her. The elemental moan snicked through her and suddenly her senses sharpened. She scanned the area inch-by-inch until her gaze landed on something that didn't fit.

Something shiny.

She stooped to pick it up—a metal ring. Frowning, she quickly palmed it.

Clay rose, asking, "You're sure this is the place?"

"Positive. Jacy called it in when she found Jeff. I came out with the wagon to bring him home. Why do you question the location?"

"I don't get what Jeff would be doing here, scrambling along these rocks on a horse. And try as I might, I don't get a sense of death here."

"What? What's going on, Clay. You were never psychic...except a little with me."

"Not psychic. Grandfather called it Navajo magic. Tuning in to nature, reading the signs...the elements."

"I saw Jeff and his horse sprawled out right there," Siobhan said, pointing to the very spot. "Both dead."

"I believe you."

"Then what's the problem? Why the doubt?"

"Look at the rocks. It appears as if nothing has moved here. If he'd been riding and the horse had slipped, there would have been an avalanche of debris. Rocks and dirt and sand. I just can't see it."

"The accident happened four months ago. You said yourself the weather—"

"You may be right. Jeff might have been tossed off the horse and landed on his neck. All nice and neat. And then the horse just could've twisted his leg and it snapped and he went over easylike."

Realizing how unlikely that sounded, she squeezed the metal ring until it bit into her hand. "But you don't buy it."

He shook his head then focused on her clenched fist. "What do you have there?"

Unfurling her fingers, she showed him. "It's one side of a grommet. It had to have come from Jeff's boot. I noticed it was gone when we brought him home in the wagon. Afterward, I didn't give it another thought."

"You have the other half?"

"No."

"Let's look for it."

Together they searched the surrounding ground. If the other half of the grommet was somewhere in the immediate area, it remained elusive.

"So what do you think this means?"

"If you don't have it with the boot and if it isn't here, that leaves one other place."

"Where?"

"Wherever your husband was actually murdered."

SIOBHAN WAS STILL PALE and quiet as they rode home. Clay had kept himself from taking her in his arms to soothe her. He might wish she felt better, but he wasn't about to be backup to the man she'd chosen over him.

As they neared the barn, he saw a black SUV driving off the property. "Whose vehicle?"

"Early Farnum." Siobhan frowned as she followed the vehicle's progress. "I wonder what he wanted this time."

They found out soon enough. Jacy was working in the barn, straightening out the tack room, still a mess after the other night. Siobhan went straight to her.

"Jacy, I just saw Early. What did he want?"

"To apologize for driving off without you last night," Jacy said.

There was a false ring to the statement, but Clay couldn't put his finger on why. Had Jacy made that up? Or had Early used that as an excuse to get on the ranch property again for some unknown reason? Maybe

Jacy had stopped him from venturing farther onto the spread.

"Nothing else?" Siobhan asked.

"That was it."

"Were you in the barn when he got here?" Clay asked.

"No, but he said he was only cooling his heels for a few minutes. He said he would be glad to wait for you, Siobhan, however long it took. I told him you weren't interested in him and that he should give up on you." When Siobhan gaped at her, Jacy quickly added, "Well, don't look at me like that. You aren't interested, only you won't be direct. Time the poor fool got it through his head to leave you—and this ranch—be."

"So how angry was he when he raced out of here?" Clay asked.

Jacy shrugged. "Fair to middling. He'll get over it."

"I kind of did tell him the same yesterday," Siobhan said, "if in a nicer way. That's the reason he drove off without me. I wish you had kept out of it, Jacy. I was trying to keep decent relations with him since he's our closest neighbor."

"Well, of course you wish I had," Jacy said. "Because you're the perfect one, the one who can do no wrong, who can't ever look bad to anyone."

"Jacy!"

"Isn't it the truth, Siobhan? You do what you want, when you want, with whom you want—" She looked straight at Clay on that one. "And you always come out seeming like the perfect lady."

"Hmm," Clay muttered, "not sure I remember that Siobhan."

Giving him a glare, Siobhan said, "Jacy, you're upset."

"What if I am? I have reason to be upset. My brother died and instead of leaving the ranch to family, he left it to someone who is running it into the ground."

"That's not fair."

"A lot of things aren't fair. This is the Double JA. I'm a J-A—Jacy Atkinson. You didn't even care enough about Jeff to take his last name! You didn't even love him!" With that Jacy stalked off, saying, "I'm going to ride out and meet the boys, see how they're doing. They found another piece of fence down and are repairing it. I want to check on the stock, see if we lost any more cows."

A stunned-looking Siobhan watched her leave the barn. "Wow!"

"She had a lot on her mind," Clay said, suddenly realizing there was some real unrest between the women. "I wonder what set her off."

"Probably something to do with Galvan."

"You could be right."

Or not. He'd heard a deep-seated anger for Siobhan in Jacy's words.

Anger that had been stewing for some time.

CLAY SAID HE WOULD TAKE care of the horses and then go back to his cottage to take a shower before lunch.

Siobhan went back to the house to get food together. Not that she was hungry. But eventually the men would need to eat and would come inside looking for lunch. She quickly put together a pot of chili, and while it was cooking, she set out bowls of toppings—shredded cheese, chopped onions and sour cream—then prepared a loaf of garlic bread and tossed it in the countertop oven on a timer.

When everything was laid out, she retreated to her bedroom, took a fast shower, then threw herself on the bed for a while, the months of trouble on the spread, starting with Jeff's supposed accident, whirling through her thoughts.

Clay had been right. The area where Jacy had found Jeff hadn't looked like the site of an accident. Maybe he was correct about the grommet, as well. Forcing herself off the bed, she went to Jeff's closet, separate from hers. She'd never touched his. Had never given away his clothes.

Or boots.

She found the work boots directly. Fetching the metal ring she'd found, she matched it to the hole in the leather. What had happened to the other half? She checked the inside of the boot to see if it had fallen inside. Empty.

Maybe Clay had been right about that, as well, that the only other place it might be was wherever Jeff had been murdered.

But if so, who'd had it in for Jeff and why? Would someone really kill him to get the ranch?

Before she could mentally go over what she knew or suspected, a banging at her door made her start.

"Siobhan, you gotta call the vet!" Ben yelled through the panel.

She ran to the door and opened it. "What now?"

"It's the horses in the corral." A distraught Ben tore at the hat he held in both hands. "They have diarrhea and it's bloody. It's bad, Siobhan, real bad. Clay was coming to the house for lunch when he checked the corral and saw them."

"What happened?"

"He found bits of oleander leaves in their sliced apples and carrots. He and Esai are workin' on getting it out of 'em, but they don't have the right drugs."

"Go help them and I'll be right there as soon as I call Doc Riddley."

Ben was already on his way. He yelled over his shoulder, "Clay said to tell you Warrior might not make it."

Clenching her jaw so she wouldn't cry, Siobhan picked up the phone and called the vet, then turned off the stove before running to the barn.

Hardly able to grasp that someone had actually poisoned her beloved horses, she vowed to do anything to save them.

Chapter Ten

"His heart rate is still accelerated—150 beats per minute." Shaking his graying head, Doc Riddley patted Warrior, who was swaying on his feet and bleeding from the nose.

Clay blew out a breath. That was more than triple what it should be. They'd had to put Warrior in a stall in the barn. He was already hooked up to an intravenous feed of lidocaine that would slow his heartbeat, and Siobhan was preparing a bag of fluids that the vet had brought to flush out the toxins.

"He's going to be all right, won't he?" Siobhan asked, her hands shaking as she unwound the tubing.

The vet gave her a kindly smile and an I-hope-so shrug. "We've got to be positive."

"I can't stand it if they d-don't all make it!"

The break in Siobhan's voice got Clay where he lived. Knowing horses were her passion, that this incident was enough to undo her, he wanted nothing more than to take her in his arms and tell her it would be okay, that all the horses would be fine.

And most of them would be.

Before Doc Riddley drove up, he and Siobhan and Esai and Ben had worked on saving the four affected horses. Induced vomiting and gastric lavage helped reduce the absorption of the toxic compounds in oleander, one of the prettiest and deadliest plants around—not that he'd seen any on the Double JA property itself. The other three horses were still in the corral behind the barn with Esai and Ben seeing to them. Warrior was by far the worst off of the bunch, the only horse that needed extreme measures. Apparently, he'd eaten more of the deadly leaves than had his companions.

"What about getting Warrior to that new hospital outside of Santa Fe?" Clay asked.

Whatever it took to save him.

"If it makes you more comfortable," the vet said. "But we don't need to run tests to figure out what's wrong with him, which would be the main reason to get him there."

"Luckily I found the oleander leaves in the feed. If we hadn't come back when we did..." Clay was just glad that they had. "So you think we can handle it?"

He covertly glanced at Siobhan, who still wasn't herself. For the moment, she didn't look as though she could handle anything stressful. He was confident she would come around, though, because that was her nature.

"At this point, I'm not sure what the vets at the hospital could do more than the two of you," Riddley said, "considering your combined knowledge of horses. Plus, you're Warrior's person," he said to Siobhan, "and your being with him goes a long way for his recovery. Besides, you've worked with horses all your life, and with that fancy degree, you know nearly as much about equine care as I do."

"But I'm not a vet."

"You're the next-best thing," Riddley said. "I have every confidence in you. I'll leave all the meds and supplies you need. You call me if Warrior gets worse and I'll hightail it back here."

Warrior didn't even look like the same horse. He was in shock, barely aware of them. His nose was still bleeding, his mucous membranes were oddly pale, and every few minutes, his sturdy body was wracked with a fine tremor.

"What should we expect for this guy?" Clay asked.

"You should be seeing a difference in his heart rate shortly. And then it's simply a waiting game. Keep him hydrated with the intravenous fluids. They'll continue to deplete the toxins. He probably won't eat until he's on the mend, so don't worry about that until morning. Maybe not even then. Keep him awake at least until his fever is down. Don't let him sleep too soon, or he could slip into a coma."

Siobhan nodded her agreement to everything, but Clay couldn't miss the fine quiver, not only of her hands, but also of her whole body. She was terrified, and it didn't look good on her. He'd never seen her so shaken before.

"Thanks, Doc," Clay said as the vet hauled his bag to the truck. "We'll keep in touch."

He turned back to Siobhan, who was checking the intravenous line and talking softly to Warrior. As she worked, he could see her mental attitude shift from scared to determined. Now that was the Siobhan he knew. When she slid her hand along Warrior's left jaw-bone, he knew she was seeking the major artery that would let her check his pulse.

"Don't you think it's a little soon?" he asked, not wanting her to be disappointed.

"Maybe," she said, glancing over to the stable clock.

Clay's gut tightened and then relaxed when he saw her expression smooth out.

"It's working. Down to 132."

Making himself comfortable on a hay bale across from the horse's stall, Clay echoed the vet. "Now we wait."

Ben entered the stable. "Hey, I was just going to get something to eat. Esai's keeping an eye on the other horses and I'm going to bring food back for him. Can I get either of you anything?"

Siobhan shook her head. "I couldn't eat. Clay?"

"I can wait a while. Maybe you'll feel like eating then, too."

"There's garlic bread in the countertop oven," Siobhan told Ben. "It'll be cold but I'm sure it's still edible."

Ben left and Siobhan joined Clay. She perched on the bale but held herself stiffly upright.

"Relax, would you," Clay said, pulling her back toward him.

She turned in his arms and would have landed on him if she hadn't put out a hand to brace herself against him. Her fingers splayed across his chest burned. The fire spread. For a minute, he thought she might kiss him again—he recognized that glimmer in her eyes. He was tempted to do the honors, but if his lips touched hers, he might never let her go.

As if suddenly awakening, Siobhan blinked and pushed herself away from him, then scooted across the bale so fast she nearly fell off.

Clay caught her forearm and saved her the indignity. "Whoa, easy there. I know you're upset but—"

"Of course I'm upset." She wiggled back up onto the bale. "Who would do this, Clay? Who would want to kill a bunch of innocent horses?"

"Who had access to the barn?"

"Early Farnum. Jacy thought he was only here for a short while, but it might have been long enough."

"He could have laced the feed," Clay agreed, "and when I let the horses into the corral it would have been waiting for them. Esai and Ben came in just as I was leaving, so their horses went in shortly after. Unless Farnum confesses, there's no way we can ever know for sure."

Siobhan looked at Warrior then out to the corral at the other horses that had been poisoned. "Maybe there is."

Clay knew she meant reading the horses in hopes that they'd seen the guilty person.

After checking out Warrior's vital signs, Siobhan appeared ecstatic. "Big improvement. His heart rate is down to seventy and his temperature is almost normal." She stroked the horse's nose and looked into his eyes. "Eyes are nearly clear."

Siobhan kept her gaze locked with Warrior's for an

interminable moment. The horse continued to focus on her, yet Siobhan sighed and appeared frustrated.

"It's all right, Warrior," she murmured, rubbing her cheek against his. "You just get well, okay? We can talk later."

Clay waited until she left the stall. "Nothing, huh?"

She shook her head. "At least he's getting better." She looked at him thoughtfully. "You're his person, too, you know. He remembers you."

"So you have read him." The fact that she'd shared his experiences with Warrior made Clay feel even closer to her. "Maybe you can get something from one of the other horses. C'mon, let's go out to the corral."

Esai and Ben sat on the fence watching the sick horses.

"They're coming along," Ben said. "A couple days and they'll be as good as new."

"If I ever get my hands on the one that did this…" Esai grumbled.

Though Clay had some ideas of what he would like to do to the bastard responsible, he didn't share them lest he work up the old hand. Or himself. It had taken work to learn to curb his temper. If he didn't keep it in check…he didn't want to think of what he might do to the responsible person.

"Why don't you guys take a break," Clay suggested.

"I'd like to check the horses over myself," Siobhan added. "We don't all need to be here."

"Sure." Ben jumped down from the fence. "I could stretch my legs. C'mon, Esai. Let's put a pot of coffee on. It's gonna be a long night."

When the two men were out of earshot, Siobhan said, "Thanks. I'd rather not have an audience."

"Figured. Want me to leave, too?"

"No, of course not." She sounded surprised that he'd asked.

Clay settled himself on the fence to watch Siobhan address the three horses one at a time, first checking them over physically before trying to make that mental connection. She spent enough time at it, kept her expression unreadable. Though he wanted to know what she was seeing, he didn't say a word lest he throw a wrench into the process.

In the end she didn't have to say anything. Disappointment was clear in her expression.

"No connection?"

"That's not the problem. They simply didn't see anything. The carrot-apple mix was already out here when they were put in the corral, just as you suggested."

IT WAS A LONG NIGHT.

Because Siobhan determined the corralled horses were past the crisis around midnight, she sent Esai and Ben to the bunkhouse to get some sleep. Jacy hadn't come back from wherever she'd gone off to, so it was up to Siobhan and Clay to watch over Warrior to make sure the horse didn't fall asleep too soon. They took turns, one napping on the bale of hay while the other kept vigil.

It was sometime in the middle of the night when Siobhan awoke to see Clay in Warrior's stall, cradling the horse's head in his hands, chanting something too low for her to hear—something his grandfather had taught him, perhaps. Watching from the cover of dark, she saw how Warrior responded to Clay, nickering softly and pushing his nose into Clay's chest. Then Clay reached up and pulled Warrior's head against him and murmured something into the horse's ear. The love between man and horse was too clear to deny.

It was a moment that stood still in time. Siobhan's heart tripped a beat and she felt the blood rushing through her veins. Seeing Clay like this with her desperately ill horse touched her so deeply that she could hardly breathe. Horses were her passion, and unless she was mistaken, Clay's feelings for his equine charges went deeper than she'd ever guessed. And it was obvious to her that Warrior was irrevocably bonded to the man who had gentled and trained him.

Just as she was now bonded to them both.

It was that moment that drove home how much she still loved Clay Salazar.

Now what would she do with the knowledge?

The prophecy still hung over her head like the sword of Damocles. It could come down on her—or rather Clay—at any moment. She already lived with the guilt of Jeff's death—surely it couldn't happen again.

Realizing Clay was leaving Warrior's stall, Siobhan flashed her eyes closed and feigned sleep. His footsteps drew closer and she felt the bale shift slightly with his weight. Her heart thundered so hard and fast, she feared he could hear its beat. But if he was aware of her physical response to him, he kept it to himself. Gradually her heart slowed and she was able to think more clearly.

She couldn't help herself.

Allowing her mind to open, she searched for him, for the connection they used to share. Again she hit a wall, which made her feel a little lost.

That connection had been a part of them. It had made them who they were together. It had made them one.

Confused, Siobhan didn't know what to think. That, indeed, Clay was safe from the prophecy?

Or that he was no longer open to love, at least not with her?

Chapter Eleven

Siobhan was relieved that by dawn the horses in the corral were eating. Though Warrior's heart rate and temperature were back to normal, he still turned away from the food bucket. She had to keep reminding herself what Doc Riddley had told her. She simply had to wait.

Nothing she could do would rush the horse's recovery.

What she could do now that she didn't have to be at the horse's side every moment was face down Early Farnum. Which was her plan directly after breakfast.

"Are you sure you want to face Early alone?" Jacy asked.

Siobhan didn't know when her sister-in-law had returned to the ranch or where she'd been the night before. Jacy had simply showed up at the house in time for breakfast and had been appropriately shocked that someone had poisoned the horses right under their noses. She'd admitted she'd put the feed buckets out before running an errand, so Early had unsupervised access to them at least for a short time.

"Siobhan won't be alone when she goes to see Farnum," Clay said. "I'll be with her."

"You and who else? Early has at least a dozen hands working for him on that spread."

"What do you think he might do?" Siobhan asked. "Have his men kill us and bury us where no one will find us?"

"Fine, joke all you want, but there's nothing funny about this situation, Siobhan," Jacy said. "I never would have guessed Early Farnum was behind any of what's been going on around here, but if he has been…then he's a very dangerous man. Who knows what he'll do to you?"

Realizing her sister-in-law was simply worried for her welfare, Siobhan said, "Thanks for the warning," but still headed for the back door. "Clay?"

"Right behind you." He took a big swallow of coffee and then followed.

Siobhan felt a little weird with him now. Her middle-of-the-night emotional discovery should have brought them closer, but the aftereffect was just the opposite. He put her nerves on edge. Part of her wanted to talk out what she was feeling with him, while another part thought she was being ridiculous.

Clay hadn't made any declarations of love…like…or otherwise.

She still wasn't certain why he'd come to warn her or why he'd chosen to stay if only for a while, but she put it to some lingering sense of obligation.

They were in his truck, heading off the property, when he said, "Jacy could be right, you know. Farnum could be dangerous. If he poisoned the horses, chances are he's responsible for the other things that have gone wrong on the spread."

"So you think I should just let it be?"

"I was thinking maybe it would be a good idea if we told Sheriff Tannen what we suspect."

"We don't have any proof, Clay. Besides, Tannen believes Jeff's death was an accident."

"Doesn't mean he can't have a change of opinion."

But Siobhan's mind was made up. "I want to speak to Early. If he poisoned my horses, I want to know it."

"I hope you can recognize the truth when you hear it."

Not wanting to argue, she didn't respond.

Early's spread was the antithesis of the Double JA. The entry was flanked by columns that supported a metal archway. The six-foot metal gates stood open, so Clay sped right through. The drive to the house was long and hilly and winding and carefully landscaped with high-desert plants. A wall of oleander graced one side of the house.

"Look at that," Siobhan choked out. Her chest went so tight she could hardly breathe. "He didn't even have to go looking for something to poison my horses."

"It doesn't look good," Clay agreed. "Farnum must have some warning system when a vehicle goes through the gates," he suddenly added. "He's out on the porch waiting for us."

Siobhan's hands tightened into fists the moment she spotted the man coming through the front door. As they pulled up to the house, she told herself to relax and to keep her temper. Try as she might, she couldn't stop her heart from pounding or her stomach from swirling, but she could put on a good face.

They were barely out of the truck when Early asked, "What can I do for you, Siobhan?" though he was looking straight at Clay with a hostile expression.

"I saw you drive off my place yesterday."

He focused on her. "I came to apologize for taking off without you the other night after the meeting. Not very gentlemanly of me."

"No, it wasn't," she said coolly. "Not gentlemanly to mess with my horses, either."

"Your horses?" Early said. "What happened to your horses?"

"They all survived. If that matters to you."

Early's brow pulled into a frown. He looked from her to Clay to her, no comprehension in his expression. Either he was a great actor or he really didn't know what she meant.

"Survived what?" he asked.

Clay finally spoke up. "The oleander leaves you mixed into their buckets of carrots and apples."

Early bristled. "Where the hell did you get the idea I would do such a terrible thing?"

Siobhan looked back at the oleander growing near the house and asked, "How long did you get to the barn before Jacy?"

"Let me get this straight." Early's face was florid and his voice rose a notch. "I went over to your spread out of common decency. To apologize for leaving you in town. Now you're accusing me of being some kind of damn criminal, of trying to poison your horses just because I have oleander on my property? I don't have an exclusive on the plant. It grows everywhere."

"Not on the Double JA," Siobhan said, her certainty that Early was guilty quickly waning.

"Your being there right before they got sick was awfully convenient," Clay said.

"Convenient or not, I didn't do it! And I'll thank you both to get off my property. You know the way!"

With that, Early slammed back into the house, leaving them staring at each other. Neither said a word as they climbed back into Clay's truck and drove off.

Early's indignant response resonated with Siobhan. She mentally went over the brief confrontation, but if there were any chinks in Early's story she couldn't find them.

"He didn't do it," she finally said.

"I know."

"Who, then? You think whoever it was laced the buckets before Early got there?"

"Not necessarily. Someone could have been biding his time, planning on doing the damage once we were all out of the way. There was probably a half hour when no one was there when we went to get cleaned up," Clay said. "Could have been Vargas sneaking around. Or Buck. Or Galvan, for that matter."

"What if the poisoning was delayed?" Siobhan mused. "What if whoever locked me in the tack room meant to poison the horses but I spoiled that plan? And then you showed up."

"Possible."

"Whoever it was drove a black truck similar to this one. That's why I originally thought it was you."

"Like I said, that's possible."

"But you don't sound convinced. Why not?"

"Because I think the intruder that night had a different goal. I found rags and a can of gasoline near the corral."

"And you didn't say anything?"

"I didn't want to scare you."

"That's not scary…it's terrifying." Siobhan shuddered as she thought what might have happened that night if Clay hadn't been around to rescue her. "At least one of our suspects is eliminated," she said. "And if Vargas did it, then Buck is the one behind everything, starting with the bank calling in its loan before Jeff died."

"Buck likes to brag," Clay mused.

Making Siobhan think he had a plan.

AFTER DROPPING SIOBHAN off at the barn so she could check on Warrior, Clay headed for Soledad. He wanted to face Buck Hale, but in neutral territory. Going onto the man's land would be asking for trouble and there would be no one to back him up. He wasn't crazy.

Alone for the moment, he felt Siobhan's absence. It had only been a few days, but he was getting used to being with her again. Developing a dependence on her presence. He worried that was a mistake. No matter how he felt about her, Siobhan didn't feel the same. And even if she did, she trusted the family curse more than she did her own feelings.

Which made *him* not trust her in the most primal of ways.

His thoughts about their relationship were cut short when his cell phone rang. He checked the ID—John Whitehorse was calling him back.

"John, did you get something on Galvan?"

"I don't know if it's really anything you can use, Clay, but word is Galvan bought up a couple of small properties in the northeast part of the state."

"Ranches?"

"Land, as far as I heard."

"What kind of land?"

"Land that's not connected. Different counties, even."

"I don't get it."

"We're talking cheap pieces of property no good for grazing because there's too much rock."

"Whoa. Sounds like he's looking for something to make him rich. As head of the committee that reconsidered uranium mining in New Mexico—"

"He's developed a personal interest. My conclusion, too."

"No wonder Galvan is so determined to make uranium mining a reality in this part of New Mexico." Clay's mind was already roiling with the possibilities.

"Sorry that's all I got."

"You did good, John. Thanks."

"Hey," John said, "when are you gonna visit your grandfather?"

"Soon. I'll let you know. Dinner will be on me."

They talked for a few minutes about personal things,

about John's family—his wife and two kids—until Clay passed the town limits. He wound up the conversation as he parked in front of the Gecko Saloon.

Inside, he got a beer from the bartender. He didn't know the guy, so he sat himself at a table where he was willing to wait for Buck Hale to come in even if he had to close down the place.

Luckily, he didn't have that long to wait.

Within a half hour, Buck and his boys strolled in and took over the bar. Not Vargas, though.

Clay stayed put and tried to drill a hole in Buck's back with his gaze. Eventually Buck turned and glared at Clay.

"I'm surprised to see you here, mestizo."

"Where do you think I should be?" Clay asked.

"With your woman...oh, that's right, she's *not* your woman, is she?"

If Buck thought he would get a rise with the taunt, Clay refused to give him the satisfaction. He merely smiled a secretive smile, as if he knew something Buck didn't.

"You're here because you know she needs you, right?" When Clay didn't respond, Buck seemed a little agitated. "Dealing with poisoned horses is a little much for her to handle alone, don't you think?"

"How did you know the horses were poisoned, Buck?"

Buck's silence spoke volumes before he said, "Word gets around."

"Word is...you might be responsible."

"Hey, Buck, you gonna let him accuse you like that?" Buck's boy Ricky asked.

Clay ignored him and went on. "Or maybe you had Vargas do your dirty work. Where is he, anyway?"

"Now if it was *your* horses, that'd be an opportunity I might not want to miss, but *I* don't have anything against Siobhan."

"Then who does?"

"Maybe you ought to ask Jacy."

Clay started. "Why? What do you know?"

"That's all I'm saying on the matter." Buck turned his back on Clay and flagged the bartender. "Another beer."

Clay sat there a moment, practically quivering with the desire to do whatever it took to make Buck talk. But he'd learned his lesson about letting his temper get the best of him, and with Buck, at that. No way was he going to let himself slip backward.

He'd put Buck on notice. If Buck was guilty, hopefully he would slip up.

Wondering what Buck thought Jacy could tell him, Clay rose from the table and sauntered past the bully and his minions and out the door. No doubt Buck knew about Jacy and Galvan. Did the man really think the politician had poisoned their horses? He just didn't know.

Sliding into the truck's driver's seat, he pulled out his cell, thinking to see if Manny had heard anything about Galvan. He called the correctional center office. Aaron answered.

"It's Clay. Any chance Manny is around?"

"Afraid not, Clay. He's at the hospital getting patched up."

"Horse accident?"

"Fists."

Clay was already on his way.

By the time he got to the correctional center, Manny was in a hospital bed for the night. Just for observation to make certain he didn't have a concussion, the doctor said, quickly granting Clay permission for a short visit.

Clay's gut tightened with guilt when he saw Manny in that bed. He really did look like a kid all bruised and bandaged, and Clay was sure he'd put him there.

"This is because of me, because of what I asked you to do, isn't it?" Clay asked, keeping his voice low.

Manny shook his head. "It's because I was stupid. I let Dudley catch me listening to his conversation."

"He was talking to Vargas?"

Manny shook his head. "Not on the phone. One of the other guys—Pete Smith."

"So were they talking about Galvan?"

"No, but they were talking about finding uranium."

Clay's pulse jagged and he thought of the conversation he'd just had with John Whitehorse. Uranium again. "Where?"

"On Double JA land. That's your lady friend's place, right?"

"Right. Did they say they were looking for it? Or did they already find it?"

"I don't know, Clay, sorry. They were just getting into it when Dudley caught me spying on him."

So he was to blame. "I'm sorry this happened, Manny. I never should have involved you in this. I'll make it up to you if I can. What can I do?"

"The only way you can make it up to me is when you're done helping your friend...come back here and teach us what you know. We need you."

His feelings about the situation split in two directions, Clay said, "Looks likely."

Manny's response was a happy grin sorely at odds with his bruised and bandaged face.

Before he came back, Clay had work to do.

Could what Manny overheard be right? Was there uranium on Siobhan's spread? Maybe that was why Galvan was so interested in Jacy. And why Buck had said to ask Jacy, because she had some idea of what Galvan was up to. As for his seeing Galvan and Vargas together, maybe Vargas was doing the politician's rather than Buck's dirty work.

They needed to take a closer look at Senator Raul Galvan. The only question was how?

Chapter Twelve

"We can learn more about Raul Galvan in Santa Fe," Siobhan told Clay the next morning after breakfast. As soon as they were alone, he'd brought her up to speed about what he'd learned from his contacts, and she figured going to Santa Fe was a no-brainer. "Galvan lives there, and it just so happens there's an invitation-only gallery opening tonight. I checked to see if he was invited, and he was."

"How can you be sure Galvan will show? And how do you know he was invited?"

"Teyo Ayala is a famous Southwest artist," she said. "An invitation to the private opening of such a prestigious show is something that anyone who wants to be seen—like a politician—can't pass up. I know Galvan was invited because my cousin Aislinn McKenna runs the gallery—he sent his RSVP and said he was bringing a guest, whom I assume is Jacy."

Siobhan was still unsettled that Buck had indicated her sister-in-law knew more than she was saying about the horses being poisoned. She simply couldn't figure out how to bring it up without insulting Jacy. What if

Buck was just blabbing to put the spotlight on someone else? After all, what would Buck know about Jacy's business? As far as Siobhan remembered, they'd never even been friendly.

Clay asked, "I don't need a penguin suit, do I?"

Siobhan tried to imagine Clay in a tux rather than in jeans and a T-shirt. "In Santa Fe? Glitzy casual is as fancy as people get for these things."

"Just checking."

Glad that Clay didn't fight her on this, Siobhan spent her morning going over bills. After lunch, she made one last check on the horses before getting ready for the opening. She was relieved to see Warrior eating as though he hadn't been close to death such a short time ago.

She ruffled his mane. "Hey, that's my boy."

Snorting, Warrior shoved his head into her chest. She wrapped her arms around his neck and pressed her forehead to his. She wanted in the worst way to share an image of the carrot and apple feed in hopes that she could discern whether he saw anyone tamper with it. But fearing she'd set back his recovery, she settled for an image they would both like: Clay.

Warrior nickered softly and Siobhan linked to a memory...

Clay talking to a belligerent kid...coaxing him toward the horse...

...the kid finally allowing the horse to sniff his hand...his mouth softening into a reluctant smile...

Siobhan's eyes filled and she blinked so quickly the

image dissipated, but not before she realized Clay had a real talent for what he did. He obviously loved his work.

He'd been that kid once, but something or someone had turned him around. She'd seen the change in Clay for herself. Now he was changing other lives, and she felt selfish for taking him away from that.

It was only temporary, she reminded herself. Clay would be returning to the life he loved soon.

Why did that knowledge make her feel worse?

SIOBHAN DRESSED UP HER long purple skirts, teal top and sandals with a modern tourmaline and silver squash-blossom necklace and matching bracelet and earrings. Her red-brown hair hung loose, blanketing her bared shoulders and back. She hadn't gotten this dressed up in what felt like years. She'd even spent some time putting on makeup.

When she left her bedroom for the living area, Clay was already waiting for her. His eyebrows shot up and he gave her a low whistle.

"Don't you look spectacular!"

Siobhan felt heat rise to her cheeks, but she didn't mind. It was nice for once to feel like a woman rather than a ranch hand.

"You're not bad yourself. This looks a whole lot better on you than a penguin suit would."

Clay wore brown trousers and a light brown suede sports jacket with a Native American design burned into the back yoke. He was wearing a T-shirt, which seemed to be his signature, though this one was a tan silk that set off his sun-warmed features.

He took away her breath, and from the look he was still giving her, she knew he was feeling the same way.

They drove halfway to Santa Fe with the radio blasting. Siobhan put up with it for a while then finally turned it down to conversation level.

"So, what if we suspect Galvan's guilty?" she asked Clay.

"We need some kind of proof."

"I can't imagine how we're going to get that."

"If we can find it, we can steal it."

"Clay! That isn't funny."

"I'm not joking. Someone not only tried to kill your horses, Siobhan, he succeeded in killing your husband. He tried to kill me. And he's trying to drive the Double JA into dust. We can't let someone like that just walk. We do whatever we have to."

"I don't want to let him walk. I also don't want to cost you your job." Siobhan imagined he would lose it if they got caught and charges were brought against him.

"Let me worry about that."

"I'm already worried. I know how much you love your work, how much it means to you."

He gave her a swift look. "Now how would you know that?"

"You have to ask?"

"Warrior? That horse doesn't know when to keep his thoughts to himself."

"He loves you, Clay. I'm sure all the horses you gentle do. I love that and don't want to see it destroyed."

The closest she'd come to admitting how she felt about him. She couldn't be direct. She had to keep something—even if it was only a horse—between them.

"So what do you want me to do?" he asked.

"Be careful."

"I'm not the hothead I once was."

"I know that. But I still think you would do anything for something you cared about."

"Or someone," he added. "Is that wrong?"

"No, I just don't want to take advantage. And I can't help wondering why…I mean after what happened… the way I treated you…"

"I've come to understand fear, Siobhan. It comes in many guises."

She knew he was thinking about the past, about her ending their relationship when they were madly in love. "I wasn't afraid to love you…not the way you mean it."

"No, you had to use a family curse as an excuse."

"It's not an excuse. The prophecy is real."

"I'm sure you believe that."

She hadn't wanted to believe it. She'd heard the stories all her life, of course. But it wasn't until that fateful day that she'd spoken to her mother that she had been convinced beyond any doubt that a future with Clay was hopeless.

"I thought I ought to warn you that Mom will be at the opening," she said. "And she doesn't know I'll be there with you, so if she says anything…"

"Right. I remember she never liked me."

"That's not true." Realizing they were on the outskirts of Santa Fe, Siobhan said, "Aislinn will be delighted to see you again."

"Does *she* know I'm coming?"

"Not yet."

Her cousin had always hoped Siobhan and Clay would work out despite Mom's dire predictions. That would have meant Aislinn would have had a chance for happiness, too. She'd seemed shocked when Siobhan had pushed Clay out of her life, but she hadn't offered an opinion. To this day, Aislinn refused to talk about love or about the prophecy. Sadly, to this day, she'd never professed love for any man.

At least Siobhan had known what love was like.

Spending one's life alone or with someone he or she didn't love seemed to be the fate the McKennas in her branch of the family all had inherited.

Siobhan feared she was no exception.

TRAFFIC WAS HEAVY DRIVING through the plaza area, as Clay had known it would be. Though most shops were already closed, it was Friday, the night galleries had openings and weekends were big business at restaurants and bars. He zigzagged through town to the entry to Canyon Road, home to more than one hundred art galleries and studios housed in the historic adobe buildings that made Santa Fe legend.

Desert Dreams, Aislinn's gallery, was located halfway along Canyon Road. Parking in a shared lot down the street from the gallery gave Clay a little time to pull himself together. Not only was he going to have to face Siobhan's cousin but her mother, as well. He shouldn't let that bother him—he wasn't here for them—but he couldn't help remembering the way Siobhan's mother had always looked at him.

"There's a good crowd," Siobhan said as they got to the gallery entrance.

"Good for Aislinn, bad for us. It'll be a trick to get Galvan alone."

Siobhan handed her invitation to the man at the door. He checked his list then let them into the gallery. Teyo Ayala's work covered every wall in the front room. The artist himself was there, dressed in Santa Fe chic, arms and neck loaded with silver jewelry. He was glad-handing potential buyers who seemed fascinated by the man.

When Clay didn't see Galvan, he urged Siobhan to the next room with more paintings by Southwestern artists, which seemed to be the gallery's specialty.

A waitress swept by. "Champagne?"

"I'll pass," Clay said, and Siobhan waved her off, as well.

They were making their way through the crowd when a woman who looked enough like Siobhan that they had to be related—green eyes, masses of burnished dark hair—stopped in front of them. She was taller than Siobhan and sleeker of build, and her angular face had matured into a sophisticated version of the girl she'd been. Clay thought that if the art-scene gig dried up, Aislinn could make a living as a model.

"There you are!" Aislinn said, her smile slipping a bit as she got a direct look at Clay. "And look who you're with."

"Aislinn," Clay murmured.

Aislinn gave her cousin a hug…and then a questioning look.

"Clay has been helping me with the spread and other things for the past few days," Siobhan said.

"What other things?"

"The kind that have been putting me in danger of losing the ranch." Siobhan then whispered more directly into her cousin's ear, and Aislinn's eyes widened.

"Is that why you wanted to know about the guest list?" she asked, discreet enough to avoid using Galvan's name.

"Exactly."

"You will tell me everything."

"Later."

"Of course. This isn't the place." Aislinn nodded toward the back door. "You might be interested in checking out the sculpture garden."

"Okay, good, separated from the crowd," Siobhan said, then asked, "Mom isn't out there, is she?"

"No, Aunt Sorcha hasn't arrived yet."

"Good."

Clay silently agreed. Maybe they'd be able to get out of there without having to face the woman who'd always disapproved of him.

"Stay out of trouble, would you?" Aislinn pleaded softly.

"Too late for that," Siobhan said. "But we are trying to make things better, not worse."

Clay could feel Aislinn's worried gaze on them as they made it out to the small sculpture garden with large works placed around a koi pond. Indeed, the crowd was sparse out here, for the evening had turned chilly. It wasn't difficult to spot Galvan at the center of a small knot of people, Jacy right next to him. A bulky man stood to one side, his hands crossed in front of him. Galvan's bodyguard?

"Jacy looks bored," Siobhan said. "They must be talking politics."

"Well, then, let's join them."

Moving toward Galvan, Clay placed an arm against Siobhan's back then had to steel himself against old feelings that threatened to surface.

"I think you should run for national office next election, Raul," a woman wearing a black dress that set off some incredible gold jewelry inlaid with semiprecious stones was saying. "I would be happy to back you."

"Thank you, Eleanor." Galvan gave her a warm smile. "I could use your support."

"Then you are thinking of stepping up your game?" Clay asked as he made room in the circle around Galvan and pulled Siobhan in next to him.

Galvan turned to him, an annoyed expression flickering across his face and then quickly disappearing. "Thinking about it, yes." He aimed a white-toothed smile at Clay.

"And your platform?"

"Helping New Mexico out of the economic mire, of course."

"By supporting uranium mining," Clay said.

Galvan's smile slipped a bit. "My constituents need work, and uranium will bring much-needed jobs and money to the state."

"It'll also bring problems as it has in the past, especially on Navajo land." Clay had seen the result for himself after leaving Soledad. "The increase in cancer was no coincidence. And it wasn't just the miners."

"Mining standards are much different than in the past."

"Maybe that will make things less dangerous," Siobhan said, "but shouldn't we wait to make certain of that before *expanding* mining operations?"

Galvan's smile froze on his face. "Nothing is set in stone."

"But it will be, won't it?" Clay asked. "Isn't that why you've been buying property in the northeastern part of the state? Land unsuitable for cattle because of too much rock. But it has the potential for uranium."

"My investments are a personal matter, not public."

Jacy captured one of Galvan's arms and said, "Maybe we should leave, Raul."

But Clay wasn't through. "And isn't that why you're after Jacy here? Because you think through her you can get your hands on the Double JA?"

"Raul, that's not true, is it?" Jacy looked uncertain.

Galvan's face had darkened, and he signaled to the man who stood at attention nearby. "Escort this man out of here!"

"Wait a minute!" Siobhan protested. "This is my cousin's gallery. You can't kick anyone out!"

"Watch me."

Clay felt meaty hands hook around his upper arm, and he had to stop himself from fighting back. He would never forget the last time he'd gone off on someone.

"I'll leave," he said. "You can have your guard dog let go."

Galvan hesitated and then nodded to the man. "Walk him to the door."

"I'll talk to Aislinn," Siobhan said as Clay swept her toward the doorway. "She'll have her own security guards take care of this."

"No need," Clay said, reminding her, "we have some errands to run while we're here in Santa Fe. You have the exact address, right?"

Her eyes widened but she nodded as they reentered the gallery. Galvan's guard stopped and parked himself in the doorway. Clay kept going until Aislinn found them again.

"How did it go?"

"Pretty much as expected," Clay said.

"Now we're off to look for proof," Siobhan said, glancing back toward the sculpture garden. "Keep him here as long as you can." She picked up a gallery card and scribbled on the back. "This is Clay's cell number. Call when he leaves."

"Siobhan, I don't like this."

"That makes two of us. But if Galvan is behind Jeff's death—"

"What?"

Siobhan gave her cousin a hug that muffled her questions, then she headed for the front door. They were outside when they came face-to-face with Sorcha McKenna, a shorter and more mature version of her daughter.

"Siobhan, you're leaving already?" Sorcha glanced from Siobhan to Clay. Recognition hardened her expression. "Honey, what are you thinking?"

"No time now, Mom. Gotta run."

"Wait a minute!"

To Clay's relief, Siobhan grabbed his hand and dragged him down the street, ignoring her mother calling after them.

"Siobhan Rachel McKenna!"

They didn't have time to get into the family disagreement he saw coming. He only hoped they'd have the time and wherewithal to get proof that Galvan was orchestrating the Double JA's collapse.

Chapter Thirteen

Siobhan was out of breath by the time they got to the parking lot. When Clay helped her into the truck, she wanted in the worst way to put her arms around him. She'd seen how her mother had looked at him and knew that couldn't have been pleasant for him. He didn't deserve that. Not when he was putting his own life on hold and in danger to help get hers in order.

The things he'd said to Galvan added to everything else she knew about Clay, had made her heart open to him once more. Clay Salazar was the best man she knew.

As much as she hated the idea of breaking into someone's home, she just didn't see another way to find the proof they needed. Still, she didn't take an easy breath until they were back on Canyon Road.

"Which way?" Clay asked when they reached the fork in the road.

"It's close by. I can get you to El Caminito, but we'll have to look for the house numbers."

Senator Raul Galvan lived in the Eastside neighborhood that had once been considered the barrio. Now, with the historical importance of Santa Fe, the neighborhood was one of the most prestigious and wealthiest. It had long been gentrified with new multimillion-dollar homes sitting among the equally pricey old adobes and territorial-style structures. Many were set on big lots in a deeply wooded area.

"So what are you going to tell your mother about tonight?" Clay asked as he drove.

"Just that we were in a hurry. Another appointment. Don't worry, I won't be telling Mom what we're really up to." She didn't want her mother worrying about her. Or trying to stop them. "If she knows what a hard time I've been having since Jeff died, she didn't hear it from me."

"I meant about my being with you. She wasn't happy to see me, Siobhan. Obviously if you don't want her to know what's going on at the ranch, you won't want to tell her what I'm doing there."

"I'll think of something."

"I always knew she didn't like me."

"You're wrong, Clay. Mom never disliked you. She feared for you. For us," Siobhan said, her thoughts going back to the worst day in her life…

"Siobhan, you've got to stop seeing Clay Salazar before it's too late!" Sorcha McKenna told her daughter on the very day Siobhan was considering taking their relationship to the next level.

"But, Mom, I love him!"

"That's the problem. I've let it go on too long without saying anything. You have to think about what you're

doing, Siobhan, now, or you'll spend the rest of your life regretting your actions. I know what that's like. I don't want to see that boy die. And I don't want you to go through what I went through afterward."

Her mother had never talked about it before. Not openly. Not relating the details.

"How exactly did my father die?" Siobhan demanded to know.

She knew why Mom wanted her to break up with Clay, and she was desperate to figure a way around the curse. Maybe if she heard her mother's story, she would see where Mom missed her opportunity.

"What difference does it make? Vaughn died because of me. It would break my heart if you did that to yourself!"

"I know, Mom. You've never tried to scare me before, but I've heard the stories. Aislinn and I don't keep secrets," she said of her cousin and best friend. *"You never talk about my father other than to say you loved each other and he would have loved his children if he'd lived to see them born. Why don't you ever talk about him?"*

"Because the pain of losing Vaughn never went away. Nor the guilt. He died for loving me. That's the McKenna curse, Siobhan. The legacy that has destroyed this branch of the family."

"Tell me. Please."

Mom looked in Siobhan's eyes, and her expression shifted. *"All right. When I was young, I didn't believe in the prophecy. I thought no one could stop Vaughn and me from loving each other all our lives, so I threw myself willingly into your father's arms and became pregnant with you and Daire. He insisted on marrying me, and I threw caution to the wind and said yes. It started out as the happiest day of my life."*

"Wait—you did get married? You've been lying to us?"

"We intended to marry...but before that could happen...the beautiful day turned into a nightmare." Her expression darkened as she remembered. *"A storm came up out of nowhere. We were at the church, racing along the walkway to go inside. He pushed me through first."* A sob caught in Mom's throat and her eyes went hollow. *"Lightning struck him, right there in the doorway, killing him instantly."*

Siobhan dissolved inside. There was no way out, then. Mom hadn't missed it. There was nothing Siobhan could do to get around the prophecy, to stop it from taking Clay away from her if she took their relationship to the next level. Her father's death had been due to no reason other than fate. McKenna fate.

The McKenna curse.

She couldn't let Clay die because of her. She loved him too much. She knew what she had to do.

Some time later, Clay arrived to pick her up. When she looked at him, he didn't have to say a word for her to know how he felt. She could read the love written on his face.

Slowly, his smile slipped. *"What's wrong?"*

"I can't go with you, Clay."

"Did something happen?"

"Something terrible. And something equally terrible

will happen to you if you don't get away from me for good."

"What are you talking about?"

"Our love is cursed. We can't ever be together."

He sought their psychic link, tried to use it as he put his arms around her. Siobhan, you know how much I love you. And I know you love me.

Refusing to acknowledge the connection, she slipped away and said, "I'm serious, Clay. You have to go. Go and never look back!"

Again he communicated without speaking, as if he could force her to acknowledge the connection she was trying to deny. You can't mean that! I'm not going anywhere, Siobhan!

That was when she stepped back through the doorway and slammed the door in his face.

Then crumpled to a heap and sobbed her heartbreak on the Saltillo tile floor...

THOUGH SIOBHAN HAD regretted losing Clay, she'd never regretted the choice she'd made. Better to break his heart than to be responsible for his death.

Clay turned onto Galvan's street.

"Slow down," she said.

The street was dark, the houses scattered on big pieces of wooded property, many hidden behind walls of piñon or adobe, the numbers difficult to see. But at last she found it.

"This one."

Clay drove a little farther to an adjoining property where several other vehicles were parked diagonally outside an adobe fence. They walked back, careful to check around them to make certain no one was watching. Though lights flickered at them through the pine trees, the area felt spookily deserted. Galvan's house was surrounded by an adobe fence, but as was typical in the area, there was no gate.

They slipped inside. A huge patio was surrounded by a lush garden that fronted two attached buildings—an original century-old house and a newer casita, probably a guesthouse.

"No dogs," Clay said, keeping his voice down.

"Thankfully. Where do we start?" Siobhan's stomach roiled at the thought of breaking into someone's home.

"Stay here and let me look for an alarm system."

Using the flashlight he'd brought from the truck, Clay carefully started checking the windows of the main house.

Alone for a moment, she wondered if it was too late to change her mind. She'd never done anything like this before, but she had to admit she was getting desperate. If they didn't resolve this situation soon, she would lose the ranch, not to mention the possibility of losing her life, as well.

"Can't see any signs of an alarm system," Clay said softly. "Let's check for an open window or door."

Siobhan could hardly breathe as she crept along the casita, trying to find a way in, while Clay took the main house. She stood on the small covered porch that was like an outdoor living room with upholstered love seat and chair. Surrounded by myriad pots of flowers and cacti, she followed her instincts and lifted the pot closest to the door.

"Clay!" she called in a loud whisper, removing the key from beneath the pot. "Look what I found."

He was at her side in a minute.

They were inside in seconds and quickly dismissed the casita as holding nothing of interest. A long hallway connecting the addition to the main building led them into the living area of the house. The focal point of the viga-ceilinged room was a kiva fireplace in one corner of the white-plastered walls. They crossed through the room filled with leather couches and chairs and pine tables to a smaller hallway where they opened doors until they found Galvan's home office.

As she entered, Siobhan said, "I wish we knew what we were looking for."

"Anything that has to do with uranium."

Information on uranium mining turned out to be most of what they found in his file drawers and in the folders on Galvan's desk. One wall held a map of New Mexico with existing and potential mines marked off.

"Nothing in the Soledad area," Clay said.

Which made Siobhan wonder for a moment if they were on a wild-goose chase. But she kept up the search, and a few minutes later, she found an oversize envelope in the desk's middle drawer.

"Wait, what's this?" Slipping the contents out of the envelope, she put aside the letter on top and took a good look at the contents. "Plats of survey...I think of that land Galvan bought."

At her side in a second, Clay swore under his breath and pulled his cell phone from his pocket.

"Aislinn." He answered, listened for a few seconds then said, "Thanks," and slipped the cell back into his pocket. "Your cousin stalled Galvan as long as she could, but he's on his way. We have to hurry. Start turning off lights."

Siobhan's chest went tight, but she nodded and turned off everything but the desk light.

Together they spread the envelope's contents across the desktop. Siobhan was so nervous, she had trouble focusing her mind on what was before her eyes. Then one plat in particular took her attention.

"This is the Double JA! He has a plat of the ranch! And look at this." She pointed to an area marked out in red. "What do you think that means?"

"That he thinks he can find something in that area— like uranium?" Clay picked up the letter. "The letter's addressed to Galvan and it details the plats he requested. Proof that he's after your property."

"Let's take it."

"He'll know it's missing." Clay looked around. "He has a copier." Picking up the survey of the Double JA and the letter, he rushed to the copier and turned it on. "Put the other surveys back in the envelope. We have to leave everything the way we found it."

Siobhan did as he asked. Time was ticking away. Finally the copier was ready and Clay printed the letter just as they heard a vehicle pull up.

"He's back!"

Siobhan snapped off the desk light. Her stomach

whirred in time to the copier. She thought she was going to be sick right there.

"Done! Put the copies in the envelope," Clay said, handing them to her. "If he checks the contents, Galvan won't know the letter and survey were switched until it's too late."

Hands shaking, she did as he asked and then put the envelope back where she found it.

Clay was already at the door, waiting for her. "We'll go out the way we came," he whispered.

She heard Galvan slam the SUV's door as they left the room. Her stomach clenched and she had trouble breathing as Clay rushed her into the living area. They were halfway across the large open space when she heard Galvan insert his key into the lock.

"C'mon!" Clay urged softly, pushing her.

Siobhan tripped and would have fallen had Clay not caught her around the waist. He pressed her into his side, stealing the little breath she had left. Then he half carried her the rest of the way, only letting her down when they got well into the hall that would take them back to the casita.

They were halfway there when the front door swung open behind them and Clay caught her and stopped her from moving. Siobhan expected to hear voices but all was quiet. Had Jacy gone home?

Clay urged her to move. She did so. Slowly. Careful not to make a sound. His big warm body was pressed against hers, moving in sync. Behind them in the living area, Galvan was moving around, muttering something to himself. Then noise suddenly blasted them and she started and nearly tripped over her own feet. He'd turned on the television. Luckily the sound of the basketball game was so loud, he probably wouldn't have heard no matter what they did.

At last they were back in the casita.

Shaking, she stood on tiptoe so she could whisper in Clay's ear. "Should we replace the key?"

His lips tickled her ear when he murmured, "Let's not take the chance. Maybe no one will look for it any time soon. We need to be careful when we get out there. We'll be in the open. If Galvan looks out his window at the wrong time…"

Cracking open the front door, she whispered, "Then let's go along this building into the garden. It's farther away and we'll at least have some camouflage."

"You slip out first. I'll give you ten seconds, then follow."

Siobhan's heart thundered so hard she swore Galvan could hear it as she slid along the side of the building and behind a tree. Was that a curtain she saw moving in his living area or did she just imagine it? Thinking Galvan might be watching them made bile surge up her throat. She almost choked on the bitter taste.

A glance back assured her Clay was following. Certain that at any minute Galvan would spot them and yell at them to stop, she took comfort in the fact that Clay was there with her, that he would protect her. He was a man she could count on, no matter how dire the circumstances.

She only prayed she didn't get him killed.

Chapter Fourteen

Late the next day, Clay let everyone off early enough that he and Siobhan could ride out while there was still some daylight left. Using the survey they'd taken from Galvan's study, they set out to find the marked-off area. Chief, the horse Clay had chosen to ride, had recovered enough from the oleander poisoning to work, but Warrior needed more recovery time, so Siobhan took Garnet out.

Clay didn't know how many miles they rode along the dry creek bed lined with cottonwoods, but eventually they reached sandstone. He stopped and took out the survey. Siobhan pulled Garnet up next to him and leaned in so she could see it, as well.

Aware of her closeness, of the warmth of her leg pressed up against his, he had trouble concentrating for a moment.

"This area sure can't be used for cattle," she said, jarring him back to the situation. "And looks like the marked-off area, right?"

He focused back on the survey. "It's the place of

interest, all right. To investigate further, we'll have to leave the horses here."

They dismounted and looped the reins over a low branch of a cottonwood. What he wasn't about to leave was the rifle he'd insisted on taking. They could be walking into a dangerous situation for all he knew. He'd wanted to order Siobhan to stay behind, to let him do this himself, but she'd never been good at taking orders.

They set off on foot, traveling deeper into the canyon where the sandstone walls and rims were laced with oak brush that provided food and shelter for mule deer, elk and turkey. It was a bit of a walk and they were in the open, definitely at risk.

Clay's instincts kicked in and he tuned in to his senses. His nerves sizzled, but he heard nothing unusual, and when he looked around, he saw no apparent sign of danger.

Suddenly he realized Siobhan had grown really quiet. Because she was considering the possibility of finding uranium on her land...or was she thinking about the husband she'd lost?

The reminder made him pull back. He needed to stay on an even keel emotionally. He needed to remember he couldn't trust her when it came to what might be going on between them. He'd seen how easily she'd walked away from him before.

They were close to finding some answers; therefore, he needed to keep a clear head, which meant he had to keep his thoughts on their search.

As the ground beneath their boots shifted from sand

to sandstone, Siobhan asked, "What exactly are we looking for?"

"I guess we'll know it when we see it."

Clay swept his gaze over the rocky terrain that gradually rose higher up the side of a hill. What to look for—that really was the question. But as they penetrated the area farther, each exploring a different area, it didn't take long to come up with an answer.

"The rock over here looks like it's been tampered with," Siobhan said.

Clay looked over the expanse before Siobhan. Rather than sitting in big formations as though they'd been there for hundreds of years, chunks of smaller pieces littered the ground.

"Looks like someone took a pick to the sandstone," he said, "which probably means that someone was searching for uranium here."

"And uranium looks like…?"

"I've never seen it myself," Clay admitted, "but I understand uranium-bearing ore can have a yellow or brownish hue."

Having set down the rifle, he was already sorting through the pile, examining chunks that were fist-size and larger. Nothing and more nothing.

A few yards away, Siobhan was doing the same. When she made a noise that was somewhere between a gasp and a choke, he quickly dropped the rock he was inspecting and went to see what she had found.

It wasn't a rock with yellow ore in her hand. Instead, she held a small metal ring like the one found at the site where Jeff Atkinson had supposedly died accidentally.

"The other half of the grommet," Siobhan said. "Looks like you might be right, then. Jeff at least had to have been here the same day he died—once the grommet came apart on his boot, the other side wouldn't stay put for long. But why was he here in the first place?" she asked softly. "And if he did die here, why would the murderer move his body up near the rimrock?"

She looked at Clay as if he could provide the answer.

Clay tried to imagine how exactly Jeff Atkinson had been killed, but he came up blank. Jeff's neck had been broken. More than likely it had happened here, because he couldn't see the man willingly following his murderer to a more convenient location, couldn't imagine the killer taking the chance that Jeff could get away unscathed. He imagined the killer had done whatever was necessary to break his horse's leg once they got near the rimrock to make the "accident" seem all the more believable.

"I would guess the murderer—maybe Galvan himself—didn't want anyone investigating this area too closely," Clay suggested. "If there is uranium here, then everything falls into place. I think we keep looking."

"That makes two of us," Siobhan said, her expression determined.

Clay turned his gaze to the rock around him. He didn't want to see the love for her late husband etched in Siobhan's expression, so he avoided looking at her. Helping her find Jeff's murderer was taking an emotional toll on Clay. On the one hand, he was opening up to her. On the other, he was forced to face again the choice she'd made to marry another man, one she had obviously loved.

Immersed in those thoughts despite himself, he whipped through a pile of broken-up sandstone. He didn't know how long they were out there, but the sun set and dusk was settling over the area when he found it—a rock with a yellowish underbelly.

This was it, he thought, the ore nearly burning his hand.

Proof!

Clay was about to show it to Siobhan when a blast from behind made him jump. Rock next to him split into shards and splattered him.

"What the hell?" he yelled, grabbing on to his rifle as another bullet just missed him.

"Clay?" Siobhan turned to see what was going on.

Acting on instinct, Clay rushed Siobhan and grabbed her tight to him as he pulled her to safety behind a jagged sandstone wall. Damn! He'd only wanted to protect her, and here he'd led her straight into danger.

The bullets kept coming.

And Siobhan clung to him as if she never would let go.

As much as he wanted to indulge himself in that thought, Clay shoved her to the ground and ordered, "Keep your head down!"

Thankful he'd been cautious enough to bring a weapon, Clay hefted the rifle in his hands and edged away from her.

"Clay, what are you doing?" she whispered.

"Trying to save our butts."

"Don't...you'll be killed!"

They'd both be killed if he didn't do something to prevent it. "I'll be fine."

"Then so will I!"

One look at Siobhan and he knew she was determined to come with him. She was already on her knees. "Stay put, Siobhan! I mean it!"

He moved sideways behind the rocks, every few seconds bobbing his head up to see if he could get a look at the shooter. Despite the fact they were using the survey Galvan had bought, he doubted the politician was up to doing his own dirty work. Vargas, then? Though the man worked for Buck Hale, he'd had something going on with Galvan the other night in town.

The rifle burned Clay's hands, made him itch to use it, but the weapon was useless if he couldn't get a clear target.

Finally he was far enough from Siobhan that he chanced taking a good look.

In the distance, a man dressed in black, lever-action rifle in hand, ran toward the stand of cottonwoods where they'd left their horses. A brimmed hat covered his head and shaded his face. It didn't look like Paco Vargas to Clay—the ex-con was far more muscle-bound than this guy.

Clay took aim and undoubtedly could have hit the man, but under the circumstances, he couldn't make himself pull the trigger. He'd never shot anyone before. He certainly had never killed anyone.

Coming close once had been enough for him.

Clay aimed at a spot between the attacker and the cottonwoods and let off a couple of shots, hoping to get him away from the horses. The man just ran faster and took shelter behind the tree. Next thing Clay knew, the horses were taking off, running wild, the attacker mounted and flat on Chief's back.

Clay let his gaze follow the direction the gelding was heading and spotted a black truck parked nearby.

The same truck Siobhan had seen the night she'd been locked in the tack room?

There were a lot of black trucks in the area, but this one was old and looked familiar, Clay thought, checking out the design of the brake lights. It reminded him of the one Buck Hale used to drive...

The attacker slowed Chief and, without stopping, dismounted near the truck, rifle still in hand. The horse ran off. Clay took a couple of more shots, but the man whipped himself out of target range into the driver's seat, started the engine and drove off. Clay aimed for the tires, thinking if he could put the man on foot, he would be able to track him and overpower him with surprise, but the truck had already gotten too far away and was moving too fast. He had to admit defeat.

Siobhan! Wanting to make sure she was all right, he turned to check on her. She was standing there right behind him, her face a mask of fury as she stared out after the fast-disappearing truck.

Despite his orders, she'd followed him.

She'd put herself in more danger!

"What were you thinking, Siobhan? You made your-self a target by coming out into the open like that! Can't you ever listen to anyone?"

"I'm not a child, Clay. You can't give me orders."

"Apparently not, even if it's to save your life!"

"It's *your* life I was worried about!" she countered.

"Don't give me that curse nonsense again!"

"It wasn't the prophecy…the connection we had is gone…but someone was shooting at you, Clay!" Her voice trembled with the knowledge. "You could have been killed. I—I couldn't stand it if anything happened to you."

Clay couldn't stand it. He couldn't stand to hear the sorrow in her tone. Couldn't stand to see her features crumple. Couldn't stand to feel her defeat. They didn't need a connection for him to know how utterly hopeless she was feeling right now.

He slid his hands over her shoulders and grasped her upper arms, resisting the urge to shake some sense into her. She wasn't a child to be chastised. She was a woman. A woman he knew he still wanted.

Unable to help himself, Clay pulled Siobhan to him and fixed his mouth to her trembling one. Seeming shocked, she tried to pull away, but he held her fast, nudged her lips open, kissed her with all the passion of a man who'd never stopped loving her.

Siobhan softened in his arms. Then, as if the years melted away into nothing, she was kissing him again with every bit as much passion as if she hadn't driven him away.

Shocked, Clay realized that even though she'd married another man, Siobhan had never stopped wanting him.

The question was, did she still love him?

FOR ONE SWEET MOMENT, Siobhan allowed herself to be lost in the kiss. She gave herself up to pure sensation, to Clay possessing her as only he could. She'd dreamed of this so many times...times she'd regretted because of the man she'd married.

Coming to her senses, she pushed Clay away. Her pulse was pounding and she was having trouble breathing. She couldn't look him in the eye.

"What are we doing?" she gasped. "We have to get out of here!"

She thought Clay might try to convince her otherwise. Thought he might try to kiss her again. Instead, he stepped back, leaving her with a sense of loss she couldn't deny.

He said, "Getting out of here will be a trick with the horses gone."

In a state of near panic caused more by her own feelings than someone taking a couple of shots at them, she looked around wildly. Both Garnet and Chief were nowhere to be seen. Undoubtedly they were on their way home, wanting to get there in time for supper.

In the meantime, she was here with Clay.

Alone.

This couldn't be. There had to be a way out of this. It was already getting dark and her mind was playing tricks on her, taunting her with what could happen between two people who'd once wanted each other more than anything in the world for much of their adult lives.

But that was then, and this was now.

"You have your cell phone on you, right?" she asked.

"Maybe a cell is something you should have since you keep needing to use mine," he murmured, pulling it from his T-shirt pocket and handing it over to her.

"I'll put it on my wish list."

Siobhan breathed a sigh of relief. She'd make a call and someone would come to get them and then she wouldn't have to make a decision she might later regret.

Or so she thought until she tried to scare up a signal.

"Nothing." She could hardly look at Clay. "We can't just stay here. What if the attacker comes back with reinforcements?" Not that she believed it, but she was trying to pretend her panic didn't come from a personal basis. "We have to get away from this area."

Clay was looking at her thoughtfully. "I suppose we can walk a ways and try again."

So they walked. She checked the cell once more when they got to the stand of cottonwood trees where they'd left the horses. No signal there, either. And it was getting dark.

"Looks like we're walking home," she said.

"In the dark? On this terrain? It'll take us several hours to get back on foot."

"What do you suggest?"

"We find a place to camp for the night and start out again in the morning."

Fearing to be alone with Clay all night, Siobhan said, "I think we should keep going. We'll get a signal eventually."

ONLY THEY NEVER DID. Over the next hour, as an inky darkness descended, they followed the dry creek bed, and she tried several times to no avail. There wasn't even a moon to guide them, and she knew they would soon have to veer off from the creek across miles of pastureland. Then they could easily get lost.

Defeated, she finally said, "I guess we'd better find a place to make camp."

Not only was it dark, the temperature was also dropping fast as it always did in the mountains after sundown. It was still spring and could get pretty cold at night.

They took refuge in the shelter of a cottonwood, which at least protected them from the wind. Clay had a pack of matches in his jeans, so they gathered dried branches and made a pile big enough to provide a fire all night. Luckily, tufts of grass softened the earth, making a decent bed.

Things could be worse, though how Siobhan wasn't exactly sure. Spending the night next to a man who assaulted her senses and made her heart ache without even trying was going to be torture.

Okay, it could be worse if they were still connected...

Trying to get her mind off the past, off the what-ifs, off the man whose arms she wished she could have holding her right now, Siobhan asked, "Did you recognize the person shooting at us?"

Busy building the fire, Clay said, "Afraid not. He was too far away. The only thing I'm certain of is that it wasn't Vargas."

"How can you be sure?"

"The attacker wasn't buff enough. Vargas is a gym rat. His muscle mass is apparent even when he wears long sleeves as the attacker did."

"Then it had to be Galvan himself," she mused. "He must have seen us leave his property last night and decided to stop us before we ruined his plans."

The thought made her shiver. She wrapped her arms around herself as though that would warm her inside.

"Even though we know Galvan is interested in expanding uranium mining and has an interest in the Double JA, he might have nothing to do with what happened," Clay said. Pulling out the matches, he lit the dried wood. Flames shot up, making a bright spot in the dark. "That should help keep you warm." He threw a few more branches on top of the pile then went on. "I thought I recognized the truck. Buck used to drive one just like it."

Buck had been one of their initial suspects along with Early Farnum, more so after he'd hired Vargas, Siobhan thought. She'd crossed off Early as a suspect, but never Buck, who'd probably held a grudge against her for the past decade. He'd hated her ever since Clay had come to town and she'd stood by him against "her own kind," as Buck had reminded her all too often.

She held her chilled hands close to the fire and took

comfort in its warmth. "Buck makes more sense than Galvan doing the shooting himself, I suppose. But still, Galvan is the one who had the survey. Do you think they could be working together?"

"You tell me. Has Buck changed enough that he would take orders from anyone?"

"I'm not suggesting he was working for Galvan. But they could be partners in crime. That would explain a lot. Galvan doing the research and taking care of the legalities, Buck doing the dirty work."

Despite the fire, she shivered again and this time Clay reached out and wrapped an arm around her. For a moment, she resisted.

"Don't fight it, Siobhan. It's going to get colder. Body heat will help keep us warm."

When he didn't release her, she tried to relax into Clay's warmth. Part of her admitted that this was what she wanted, the way it should always have been. There were so many times when she'd been content just feeling his arm around her. She'd missed that closeness…

Clay sank into a thoughtful silence.

There was a time when Siobhan had known what he was thinking, when with almost no effort at all, she could link her thoughts to his. Back then, they'd been one in every way that counted except the physical.

Siobhan couldn't help herself…she closed her eyes and concentrated.

She could sense Clay, but that was it. She couldn't break into his thoughts, couldn't hear him at will. No matter how hard she tried, she hit a mental wall.

That was good, she told herself, because it would

keep him safe from the prophecy. Even so, she mourned the loss of that special closeness they'd once had.

The thing was…it didn't keep her from loving him… didn't keep her from wanting him.

And what would having him hurt?

Now that the connection was severed, Clay was safe no matter what they might do, right?

Snuggled into his side, she could feel his heart rate speed up. His hands tightened on her possessively. A delicious sensation spread like wildfire from where they made physical contact to her very core. Heat radiated from her belly and whispered to all her secret places. Her breath grew short and her center released wet heat that made her throb and squirm and want to get closer, to let him in where she hadn't let him before.

The way things were going—now someone was trying to kill them—this could be their only chance.

He shifted slightly so one breast pressed into his side. The nipple hardened, extended, begged for attention. As if he heard, he found it through her shirt, flicked and tugged the sensitive nub and made her gasp for more. His hand shifted, smoothed the valley between both her breasts, slid down to the front of her jeans and disappeared inside. Finding the elastic of her panties, he ducked his fingers below the material, smoothed the skin of her belly and cupped her.

Breathing hard, she spread her thighs and opened herself to him. His fingers found her, teased her, tortured her. She was wet and slick and needy. With a groan, she pushed herself over him and undid the front of her jeans. He was equally quick to free himself.

He was staring at her. Though the night was black-dark, she could sense it every bit as much as his hands divesting her of her jeans, readying her for the thing she'd kept from him to protect him. She almost stopped...but his fingers were working magic on her, making her lose her reason. Her jeans were halfway down her thighs when he pulled her up over him, and all she could think about was taking him as far inside her as he would go. He pushed his tip into her entry, and she gasped as shock waves shook her. Crying out, she forced herself down so she took all of him with her slick, wet heat.

He began moving in her then, and she joined the rhythm that set every inch of her on fire. Faster... harder...deeper. Nothing was enough.

I love you, Siobhan. I've always loved you.

"I never stopped loving you, Clay," she whispered as he took her straight to the stars with him.

At least if they didn't survive whoever had tried to kill them, they would always have this.

Only when she drifted back down to earth and collapsed against his chest did she realize that Clay hadn't spoken the words of love aloud.

Only then did she realize that he'd been lying to her—that, too, without words. He'd simply been hiding the truth from her.

The connection between them was as strong as ever.

Dear Lord, the prophecy...

...I call on my faerie blood and my powers as a witch to give yers only sorrow in love, for should

they act on their feelings, they will put their loved ones in mortal danger...

Surrounded by the man she had never stopped loving, Siobhan realized what she'd just done.

Clay was a dead man.

Chapter Fifteen

Sleep was impossible for Siobhan. She drifted off a few times, but her subconscious kept tapping into the prophecy and she saw Clay killed in various ways, each more gruesome than the last.

She stopped trying to sleep.

Lying there in the dark, listening to Clay's even breathing, feeling his arm tighten around her even in slumber, she let her mind whirl, tried to seek a way out, but all she did was spin in frustrating circles that kept leading her back to the same conclusion: there was no way to avoid the prophecy. She'd known that the day Mom had told her how her father had died. The only solution was to push Clay away...and now she feared it was too late.

She feared she really had written his death warrant.

Already mourning him as the sun crept up over the horizon, desperate to be proved wrong, she shook him awake.

Groaning, Clay blinked open his eyes. When they

found her, they lit with a smile that twisted the knife inside her.

"Time to get going," she said, pulling free of him and standing. She already felt his loss.

"What's the hurry?" His smile was inviting. Seductive. "We *could* start the day out right…"

"Or we could try to get out of here before Buck or whoever it was comes back to finish us off!" she snapped.

His expression puzzled, Clay stared at her for a moment. Then he sat up, made sure the fire was out and got to his feet.

When they started walking, keeping along the creek again, Siobhan kept some distance between them.

"Is something wrong?" he asked.

Tense, worried that he wouldn't even make it back to the house alive, she said, "Last night was wrong."

"You didn't think so, then. As I remember, you seemed to be enjoying yourself."

More than he realized, Siobhan thought, speeding up. As a married woman, she'd never quite reached the same kind of ecstasy with her husband as she had with Clay. Being with the man she loved had been an unforgettable experience. But knowing what she did now, she couldn't ever repeat it—and if such things were possible, she would take it back to save Clay.

"I did enjoy the experience until I realized you've been lying to me all along." She couldn't help being angry with him. Even if he didn't believe in the prophecy, he knew she did.

"That's not true." He grabbed her arm, stopped and whipped her around to face him. "I've never lied to you, Siobhan McKenna."

"Keeping something from me is the same thing."

No quick response. She glared at Clay and saw from his expression that he knew that *she* knew.

"You forgot yourself," she said. "You didn't speak the words aloud, but I heard you just the same. The connection that puts you in danger is still there. If I had known, I never would have—"

"Are you sure about that?" he interrupted. "It seems to me you wanted what I gave you enough that you didn't worry about the niceties."

Heat seared her face and she ripped her arm from his grasp. "My mistake." She started walking again. Faster. They were almost to the sharp curve of the creek where they would leave it and cross through tougher territory. "It was the adrenaline rush after almost being killed."

Clay easily caught up to her. Wanting in the worst way to run from him, she knew that would only exhaust her.

"You're really going to use that as an excuse?" Clay asked. "You're not going to admit you wanted me, that you've always wanted me and that it was a mistake to kick me out of your life and then marry someone else?"

"None of that was a mistake. Your coming back to Soledad was the mistake. And my hiring you. I should have sent you on your way like I did four years ago!" Maybe if she did now...maybe she could still save him.

"But it's never too late, Clay. When we get back, I want you to pack your things and leave! Go back to your own life and leave mine alone."

"What?"

"You heard me!" Now Siobhan was walking so fast, she was practically jogging. Nearly breathless. Wanting in the worst way to break down and cry. She couldn't do that, couldn't show any weakness in front of Clay or he would never let her be. "Pack your things and I'll write you a check for what I owe you. And then leave for good. I don't ever want to see you again."

It was the only possible way to get him away from the danger…by getting him away from her. Even so, she died a little more inside.

Clay laughed. "You really think you can get rid of me that easily, Siobhan? You can't chase me away again. This time, I'll leave when I'm ready. Someone tried to kill *me* yesterday, so now it's personal. But don't worry, once all this is settled, when the villain responsible for everything that's been happening around here is stopped for good, then I'll gladly ride away and never look back!"

Siobhan stopped and gaped at him. Desperation gripped her. If he stayed, he would die—she knew it!— and she would be responsible. Before she could think of a way to convince him to go, a noise in the distance caught her attention—an SUV coming their way down the ragged curved dirt road a little too fast. A different vehicle, but that didn't mean anything.

Had their attacker returned to finish them off?

"What are we going to do?" Siobhan looked around wildly, but they were in the open. This time, there was no place to hide.

"Don't panic yet…" Clay's gaze was focused on the vehicle. "It's Jacy come to find us."

Siobhan tried to pull herself together, to look natural before her sister-in-law got the SUV to the bottom of the pasture. But the moment Jacy pulled up, Siobhan realized that wasn't really possible, not when she felt so sick inside.

Jacy jumped down from the driver's seat. "What the heck happened to the two of you?" Her expression was somewhere between worried and ticked. "The horses came back alone after dark, so there was no looking for you then. I've been worrying all night."

"You have reason to worry," Clay said. "Someone tried to kill us."

Eyes wide, Jacy looked from him to Siobhan.

"Whoever tried to kill us let the horses go."

"I guess we'd better get back, then," Jacy said, looking around as if she feared the villain was still out there.

"Right."

As she rushed for the passenger side, Siobhan made sure she avoided getting too close to Clay, but she could sense his seething anger. Whatever he'd been doing before to keep her out mentally apparently was no longer working. When he came up behind her, she gave him a swift warning look. He carefully avoided touching her.

She climbed into the SUV and found her sister-in-law

already in the driver's seat. It was clear that Jacy hadn't missed a thing between them, and her expression went dark. Holding herself tight, she swiftly looked away from Siobhan as she moved the SUV off and circled toward home.

Siobhan guessed Jacy figured she'd slept with Clay. She didn't look forward to what was sure to be a confrontation with her sister-in-law the moment they were alone. Actually, it was unlike Jacy to hold in anything. Siobhan didn't know why Jacy wasn't accusing her of being untrue to Jeff's memory right now.

But when they got back to the ranch, Jacy tersely said, "I'm meeting Raul in town for brunch. Assuming he hasn't gone off without me while I've been rescuing you. I don't know when I'll be back."

She let Clay off near the cabin at his request then deposited Siobhan at the house. Her anger was palpable, but for once Jacy kept what she was really thinking bottled up inside. Siobhan was simply thankful that she didn't have to deal with an emotional outburst that would most certainly drive her to tears.

CLAY COULDN'T SHOWER AWAY the bad feeling enveloping him. He'd known better than to trust Siobhan. He'd been right not to trust her all along. She was pushing him out of her life again. Only now he didn't push so easily as he had the last time. During their argument and the silent drive back, he'd felt everything she'd felt, but he'd gotten no satisfaction from her frustration or her despair.

Dressed in a clean black T-shirt and jeans, he took the rifle, which he'd reloaded, and hopped into the truck intent on tracking down a too-familiar varmint.

He and Buck Hale had been enemies forever. He didn't know if Buck had killed Siobhan's husband or if he'd been trying to make the Double JA go bankrupt, but he was certain that had been Buck's old truck he'd seen the day before. He was also pretty certain Buck wouldn't mind seeing *him* dead.

Clay had gotten the upper hand on the bastard before leaving town to find his mother's people, something Buck would never forgive...

"Do you take this man to be your lawfully wedded husband...?"

Sick inside, hardly able to breathe, Clay stood in the shadows at the back of the church and finally faced the truth: the woman he loved was lost to him forever.

"I do," Siobhan said, her expression peaceful.

"You may kiss the bride."

Gut churning, he couldn't look away as Jeff Atkinson swept his new bride into his arms and kissed her as though he never would stop.

A spattering of applause broke out, and Clay simply couldn't take any more. He headed out of the church and straight across the street to the Gecko Saloon.

"Tequila, straight up." When Tom set the drink in front of him, Clay threw the liquor to the back of his throat and smacked the shot glass back down on the counter. "Again."

"What's eating you?" Tom asked, pouring another.

"I'm here to drink, not to talk." Again he gulped the tequila. It was already burning all the way down his throat to his gut, but at least he knew he was still alive. "Just keep them coming."

"I'll leave the bottle here and let you help yourself," Tom said. "I hope you have someone who can drive you home." He held out his hand. "Your keys."

Clay slapped them on the counter and poured himself another shot. It didn't take long before he'd had enough to dull the pain, to nurse his broken heart, at least temporarily.

It was finished, then. He'd spent the past two years trying to win back Siobhan. He hadn't even stopped when she'd started seeing Atkinson. He hadn't stopped no matter how many times she'd told him they were through. He'd known she loved him. But apparently, he'd been wrong.

"Well, if it ain't the loser mestizo."

The hair on the back of Clay's neck stood straight when he recognized the voice of the man taunting him. He stiffened and closed his eyes and told himself to ignore Buck Hale, who stepped up to the bar next to him and took in the half-empty tequila bottle.

"Trying to drink away your sorrows?"

Clay ground his jaw closed and refused to let the man bait him.

"Siobhan made for a hot bride, didn't she?"

"Hey, Buck," Tom said, "take it easy over there."

"I'll have what he's having," Buck said.

Through his tequila-driven haze, Clay thought how Buck never actually used his name. If he called him anything, it was mestizo. It had been that way since high school. How did a kid learn to hate so completely and without reason?

Buck took the shot glass Tom handed him and filled it from Clay's bottle. He held the drink up to Clay like a toast, asking, "So what're you gonna do tonight, mestizo? You know, when Atkinson's poking Siobhan beneath the sheets?"

Without even thinking, Clay slapped the drink away with one hand and threw the first punch with the other. Buck tore into him, then, like a madman. But no matter how many times he hit Clay, that didn't erase the picture Buck had drawn of Siobhan with another man.

All Clay's resentment...all his rage...all his heart-break...kicked him in the gut along with Buck's fist.

A red haze enveloped Clay's mind, pure fury pushing him over the edge. He slammed a shoulder into Buck's chest and they both went flying, only Buck hit the bar with the back of his head and went slack. Clay landed on top of the man and slugged him over and over.

"You're killing him! He's already unconscious," Tom said, but Clay didn't stop until strong hands grabbed him and pulled him off.

Tom quickly knelt at Buck's side and felt for a pulse.

The bastard groaned and rolled his head and tried to open his eyes...he was still alive.

Hands continued to hold Clay captive, but he wasn't trying to move anymore. He was trying to mentally cut

*through the haze to process what his unleashed temper
had almost caused.*

*He'd almost killed Buck...and there was a part of
him that didn't care...*

CLAY REMEMBERED HOW he'd felt when he'd sobered
up. He'd been horrified. As if he'd been cut off at the
knees, both by Siobhan's actions and then, worse, by
his own.

What if he'd actually taken a human life?

That day had been the lowest point in his life. Unable
to live with himself—fearing being set off again if he
saw Siobhan with her new husband—he'd left Soledad,
had run to Navajo land to hide in shame.

At least that had been his plan.

The family members he'd never met had changed
all that. Grandfather especially had taught him many
things in addition to communicating with nature, includ-
ing how to hang on to his temper. And how to respect
himself.

But that didn't mean Clay would let Buck get away
with trying to kill him. He would use what Grandfather
had taught him about the power of the mind to get the
truth from the man. If Buck was guilty of any of it, Clay
would drag him to Sheriff Tannen and let the law take
care of him.

Stopping halfway down the drive of Hale Ranch, Clay
composed himself, let his mind relax and find its way
to a higher plane. He wasn't about to let anything Buck
said rile him. He wouldn't lose his temper again.

Taking a big breath, he continued on. Buck's truck

was sitting outside of the sprawling '50s-style ranch house. Not the old truck that Clay had seen the attacker use. Though there were several vehicles parked across from the house, the old truck wasn't among them. Clay felt a tickle of disappointment. And then dread.

What if Buck was out somewhere in the truck, causing more trouble for Siobhan?

Only one way to find out.

Taking the rifle with him—just in case, not that he meant to shoot anyone—Clay approached the house. The front door stood open, so Buck must be inside.

He rang the bell, but no one answered.

He rang again, and then called, "Hey, Buck, you in there?"

Still no answer.

But the skin on the back of his neck crawled. He pushed the door all the way open and looked inside. Nothing seemed amiss.

"Buck! Where the hell are you?"

Something was wrong.

He took a step inside and looked around at the worn furniture as old as the house itself. The walls were darkened with smoke from the stone fireplace—they looked as if they hadn't been painted in decades. Clay made his way to the hall and then to the kitchen with its boomerang-design countertops and chrome-legged oval table and chairs. The sun poured through the windows. Clay blinked. The floor on the other side of the counters next to the sink looked like red glass. Another couple of steps and he saw why.

Buck lay on his back, eyes wide-open and staring at the ceiling, a kitchen knife protruding from his chest.

He'd been dead awhile and he'd bled out on the linoleum floor.

Chapter Sixteen

Siobhan couldn't stand just sitting around alone, waiting for something to happen, waiting for the call that would inform her that Clay was dead or dying. Fetching a big bag of carrots from the refrigerator, she decided to go visit the horses, see how Garnet and Chief were doing after finding their way home in the dark.

And Warrior—she couldn't forget how close to death her poor boy had come.

When the phone rang before she got out the door, she didn't want to pick it up. She had to, though. She had to know.

The caller ID let her take a full breath: it was her mother.

"Hey, Mom, I'm really busy," she said right away, not wanting to get into an argument over Clay with her mother. "Can I call you in a couple of days?"

"Siobhan Rachel McKenna, don't you be putting me off. I expected you to call yesterday to explain yourself, and when you didn't, I called you last night. I'll have you know I left three messages."

"I didn't get them, Mom. Honest." Siobhan sighed. "I just got home so I haven't checked."

"You were with *him*, then."

Understanding her mother meant Clay, not wanting Mom to know the exact—and very *dangerous*—circumstances, Siobhan merely said, "Yes."

Her mother actually sobbed, making Siobhan wince. What was she supposed to say now?

"The poor boyo," her mother mourned. "There'll be no saving him now. I always liked him, the way he was so devoted to you and all," she said as though Clay were already dead. "I know you couldn't help yourself, darlin'. I understand how that kind of love twists you around, makes you do things you *know* you shouldn't."

"Maybe Clay will be the exception to the prophecy, Mom." Not that she really believed that, but still, she wanted to have hope. "You know my cousins Tiernan and Declan both beat the odds. Both are happily married."

Aislinn had told her all about her brother Declan's harrowing escape from death in New Orleans while saving the woman he loved. Aislinn hadn't had the details on the cousin she'd met only once in South Dakota, but he and his wife had survived terrible circumstances, as well. They were now honeymooning in Ireland.

"It's not that I don't want to believe there's a way out of the prophecy," her mother said. "But too many terrible things have happened to too many McKennas, your own father included."

"There's no helping it now, is there?" Siobhan said, forcing herself to keep an even tone when she wanted to break down and cry. "What's done is done. I can't take it back."

"No, I guess not. I'm so sorry, darlin', that I am."

Thankfully, her mother let her off the hook about Clay and Siobhan turned the conversation to her brother.

"Mom, have you heard from Daire lately?"

"No, and when I tried to call his cell phone, it was disconnected."

Her twin brother was leading the life of a gypsy, taking odd jobs and then moving on from place to place. He was *finding himself,* he'd told her. No details other than that. She knew he'd made it to the East Coast, but that had been a couple of months ago.

"Well, I'm sure he's all right," Siobhan said, trying to put a cheerful note in her tone for Mom's sake. "He'll call soon."

"And I'll get more gray hairs waiting," her mother said with a big sigh.

"Mom, I have to go. I really was on my way out to the barn to check on Garnet."

"I thought you said she's better."

"She is!" Of course her mother knew nothing of what was going on here at the Double JA. "But you know me. A worrier. Just like someone else I know."

"Point taken."

"Love you, Mom."

Siobhan hung up and took off for the barn, where she first checked on Warrior.

"Hey, how's my boy?" she singsonged to him.

His ears perked up and he snorted, then he sauntered

to the stall door and started lipping her clothing until he found the pocket where she'd stuffed the carrots.

"Okay, okay, greedy boy."

Warrior seemed to be himself again, and when she held them out he scarfed up several carrots. Siobhan's pulse began to thud as she realized she hadn't connected with the horse about the poisoning incident. She'd spared him the upset because he'd been too sick. If Warrior could give her the identity of the person who had poisoned the buckets of feed, she might be able to do something to save Clay.

Pressing her forehead to the horse's, Siobhan focused, made the intimate connection. She met Warrior on a cerebral plane, one without words but with images. She concentrated on the carrots in her hand.

In response, the horse brought her to a memory of Clay...

Clay offered the horse a carrot, but Warrior was fearful and backed off. Clay then set the carrot on a nearby barrel and backed away. Hesitant, the horse eyed the human warily as he went for the treat.

Clay repeated the bribe again and again, making Warrior follow him around the arena...

Tears filled Siobhan's eyes—he was everything a horse trainer should be—but she blinked them away. She tried again, this time implanting an image of the feed bucket filled with carrots and apples and laced with oleander.

Warrior grew restless, and the only memory she roused now was of his being deathly ill. His hide shivered in response to her touching him, and Siobhan realized she was simply upsetting the horse by making him go back to that terrible day.

She immediately let go of the image and let him mentally back off.

Chances were Warrior hadn't seen anything, either.

Wanting to check out his recovery further, she decided to take him outside and into the corral where Chief and Garnet were already waiting for her near the gate.

"How are you two?" she asked, hoping they'd suffered no lasting trauma from having to find their way home alone.

Siobhan walked Warrior around the corral a few times and, once convinced he seemed himself, felt a huge sense of relief. She threw her arms around his neck and hugged him. In response, he lipped her hair and then snorted, making Siobhan laugh.

"Silly boy," she said, kissing his velvety nose.

She next checked out Chief. He seemed sound. Relaxed. Hungry. When she pressed her cheek to his, she could see what he wanted. She gave him some carrots.

"Good boy," she murmured, turning to Garnet.

"How's your leg, sweetheart?" she asked, crouching down to check. Relieved that it looked fine—no reinjury—she stood and offered the old mare a few carrots.

That was when it hit her.

Because she'd been recuperating in the barn rather than in the corral with the other horses, Garnet hadn't been poisoned. Recuperating and safe from the poisoned buckets…but where she might have seen something…

Pulse fluttering, stomach twitching, Siobhan rested her head against the mare's. Closing her eyes, she pictured the feed bucket again. Imagined the view of the corral through the open barn doors.

It took a moment, but Garnet latched on to the image, and from there, the memory...

KNOWING HE WOULD BE SUSPECT, and not just because he'd found Buck dead, Clay called in the murder and waited for the official team to arrive. Then escorted by one of the uniformed officers, he went directly to Sheriff Tannen's office. The putrid-green walls were covered with maps of the area and a case board. File cabinets, a gigantic desk that had to be ancient and a couple of mismatched chairs were the only furnishings. Clay couldn't help but feel claustrophobic as he related his and Siobhan's quest to figure out how Jeff Atkinson had really died and whether it was connected to all the things going wrong on her spread.

"Siobhan said something about Jeff the other night," Tannen replied, "but she didn't go into all this detail."

"Because you didn't believe her. She decided we needed to find the proof before coming to you."

Clay finished his testimony. He didn't leave out anything except how they got the plat survey from Galvan's home office. He made it sound as if someone had given it to them.

"While we were out on Siobhan's property looking for this uranium late yesterday afternoon," Clay told the sheriff, "someone took several shots at us and then drove off our horses. I thought it was Buck Hale. We were stranded until this morning when Jacy came and got us. I decided it was time to face Buck, get him to tell the truth."

"How do I know you're not the one who took the knife to him to make him talk?"

"You have my word. Besides, I brought a rifle. Why would I use a kitchen knife when I could just as easily shoot him? Go ahead and fingerprint me, if you want."

Tannen grunted. "You could've worn gloves." The old sheriff stretched back in his chair, his piercing gaze on Clay. "Got any ideas on who could've done it?"

"Paco Vargas comes to mind. The ex-con Buck hired straight out of the correctional center. Maybe he and Buck disagreed on their arrangement and Vargas killed him to settle the dispute."

"Now that would have been difficult," Tannen said, swiping the long white hair away from his face.

"Difficult?"

"Considering Vargas has been cooling off in a jail cell since Friday night," Tannen said. "He got in a fight over at the Gecko and broke a chair over Curly Hanson's back. No court on the weekend, so he's being arraigned first thing in the morning."

Well, there went that theory. Not that Vargas couldn't have been responsible for some of the other things on the ranch. Like poisoning the horses.

"Vargas might not have done Buck, but jail is where he belongs," Clay said.

Just then, the desk phone rang, and the sheriff held up a hand to stop Clay. He answered, "Tannen," listened for a moment and then said, "Uh-huh. You're sure about that? Okay, then." Hanging up, he told Clay, "That was the medical examiner. He figures Buck's been dead twenty-four hours, give or take."

Clay started. "That means—"

"He's not the one who used you for target practice yesterday afternoon."

Which left Raul Galvan, Clay thought. His mind raced. He'd heard Jacy say she was meeting Galvan in town for brunch. Surely he could find the man.

"Am I free to go?" Clay asked.

"You are for the moment. Only don't go far. You're not one hundred percent in the clear yet."

Clay got to his feet and again said, "I didn't do it. You'll clear me. In the meantime, you know where to find me."

Tannen nodded. "Oh, Clay..."

"Yeah?"

"Don't be getting any more ideas about solving this on your own. I wouldn't want to see anyone else get killed."

"Me neither, Sheriff," Clay said.

Though he wasn't about to promise to stop now, after everything he and Siobhan had been through.

Driving through Soledad, Clay found Galvan's SUV. He slowed and took a good look around, parked right next to the politician's vehicle and hunkered down to wait.

He supposed he should call Siobhan, inform her of the latest development—Buck dead and Vargas behind bars, if temporarily. Only he didn't feel like talking to her just yet. He was still cooling down from that argument they'd had before Jacy had found them. Siobhan might be trying to drive him away for his own good, but he wasn't buying into that.

Eventually, he spotted Galvan coming down the street with Jacy. They'd just left a restaurant. Neither looked happy. They had to be arguing about something. Suddenly they both stopped, Galvan continuing to talk at Jacy until she shoved him in the chest away from her, jumped into her vehicle and drove off.

Galvan stalked down the street, almost seeming to have a storm cloud around his head.

Clay got out of his truck. He waited until Galvan was almost to his vehicle before stepping between him and the door.

"We have some things to settle, Galvan."

Clay could see the politician was startled to see him, but he quickly recovered, asking, "Who are you, again?"

"Clay Salazar. You remember, the other night I was with Siobhan McKenna at Desert Dreams Gallery, where we challenged you about uranium mining. You had your bodyguard escort us to the door." Clay hesitated a moment before adding, "And oh, yeah, I was the man you tried to kill yesterday."

"What are you talking about?"

"You followed us out past grazing land to the sandstone formations where you ambushed us."

"You're out of your mind!" Galvan tried pushing by him to get in his SUV.

Clay wouldn't let him pass. He focused on the

politician, caught his gaze, looked through his eyes to his soul…if he had one. Forcing everything else away, he examined Galvan with sharpened senses sort of the way he did wild horses.

"And I suppose you don't remember getting the plat survey for the Double JA? You're really going to deny you knew there was uranium ore in the sandstone?"

Galvan backed off, but Clay didn't let up his intense gaze. His hearing fine-tuned, he caught the faint hiss of Galvan's breath as he caved.

"All right, I knew about the uranium. But I didn't try to kill anyone. That's just crazy talk."

"What did you plan to do with the information?"

Galvan didn't look guilty, but he certainly looked sheepish. Clay analyzed his tone as the politician said, "It's the reason I've been courting Jacy—uranium could make a man wealthy enough to have whatever he wants."

"Jacy doesn't own the Double JA."

"Perhaps not, but she's the owner's sister-in-law," Galvan reminded him. "She has influence. I figured if there was ore on the property, she could convince the McKenna woman to let me buy that acreage. Or at least let me lease the mineral rights. Jacy didn't respond to the idea the way I'd hoped. I believe you saw how angry she just was when I tried talking to her about it."

"Romancing a woman to get your hands on uranium? What else would you do, Galvan?"

"Hey, I like money as much as the next man, but I don't break the law. I work within it. If someone was trying to kill you, then look for another reason."

Throughout Galvan's responses, Clay kept track of the man's heartbeat. It remained as steady as his voice. He was halfway convinced Galvan believed his own words.

Clay asked, "If you're such a stickler for the law, then what about Paco Vargas?"

"What about him?"

"You were arguing with the ex-con in town the other night."

"I was warning him to stay away from Jacy after she told me the man was following her. I threatened to put him back in jail if he didn't leave her alone."

Clay couldn't help but believe him. Still, he asked, "And what about Buck Hale?"

"What about him? I don't know the man, never even met him. I only know Vargas was working for him."

If Galvan even knew that Buck had been stabbed with his own kitchen knife, he sure wasn't showing any signs of it. Clay let go, let his senses return to normal. The world moved around him again. Sights, sounds, people crossing the street and getting in and out of their vehicles.

Had he come to another dead end?

Someone had shot at them. Buck had already been killed. Vargas had gotten himself thrown in jail. And Galvan was pretty convincing in claiming his innocence.

The only suspect left was the one they'd ruled out first…apparently too soon.

Early Farnum.

Chapter Seventeen

Garnet had seen it—the old mare had been witness to the whole ugly incident from her barn stall. Now Siobhan had seen the oleander leaves being added to the bucket, had seen the horses sicken after eating the poison, too.

Still stunned, Siobhan didn't know what to do. The only proof she had was the horse's memory, and that wouldn't be admissible in a court of law. In the meantime, she had to call Clay and warn him. Apparently, a cell phone had become necessary to her life, after all.

About to go back to the house to make the call, she stopped when Jacy drove up and parked in front of the barn. Judging from her sister-in-law's expression and jerky movements, she was mad as a hornet.

Warrior nickered and shoved his nose into Siobhan's spine.

"Sorry, boy, the carrots are all gone."

The horse moved closer, his chest pressed against Siobhan's back, his head draped over her shoulder, his cheek pressed against hers. She rubbed the horse's nose as she watched her sister-in-law sweep into the barn.

Barely breathing, she replayed an abbreviated version of what she'd seen through Garnet's memory.

...the workbench across from the stall...cut-up apples and carrots poured into several buckets...thick, leathery dark green leaves taken from a bag added to the mix...buckets placed in the corral...the satisfied smile on Jacy's face as she left the corral to come back into the barn...

...the horses eating...poisoned...Warrior near death...

Siobhan snapped back out of the horrid memory just as Jacy stopped in the barn, seeming finally to notice Siobhan was just outside and watching her. As Jacy came out into the yard, Warrior let out a sharp snort and backed up, signaling his alarm. Siobhan realized she'd passed on Garnet's memory to him and now he was wary of her sister-in-law, who was entering the corral.

Did the horse understand that she had almost killed him, or was he reading her emotions?

"What's up?" Jacy asked, her expression neutral. "Are the horses okay?"

Siobhan licked her lips. She wanted to lie, to walk away from the woman she obviously didn't know at all, to go call Clay and then the sheriff and end this thing. But she couldn't move, couldn't leave her precious horses with this woman who'd poisoned them. God only knew what she might do to them next.

"They're fine," Siobhan said, staring into Jacy's lying eyes. She couldn't help herself. "No thanks to you. Why did you do it, Jacy?"

Jacy's smile faltered. "Do what?"

She knew, Siobhan thought. She was trying to act

innocent, but there was nothing innocent about Jacy Atkinson.

"Why would you poison our horses?"

Jacy had mixed the oleander leaves into the buckets and then had set them out in the corral to kill the horses. What other evil deeds had her sister-in-law executed? Siobhan wondered.

Was she responsible for everything that had gone wrong on the Double JA?

"Poison the horses? Where in heaven's name did you get an idea like that?" Jacy asked, her expression appropriately shocked.

"From someone who saw you do it."

As far as Siobhan knew, Jacy wasn't aware that she could communicate with her horses. She glanced around to see Warrior staring at the woman who'd poisoned him. Siobhan sensed his combined fear and hatred.

Turning back to her sister-in-law, she asked, "Are you the one trying to destroy the ranch?"

Jacy seemed about to deny it. Then she obviously changed her mind, because her expression shifted into something truly ugly.

"It's not the ranch I want to destroy, Siobhan, it's *you*. You never loved Jeff, but still you married him. You weren't even a real wife to him."

"That's not true."

"You wouldn't even take his name!"

"I kept McKenna only with his blessing."

"Yes, of course. He would have agreed to anything to make you happy, even when you were throwing his love back in his face!"

She'd never done that. She'd done her best to be what Jeff had wanted and needed. She'd done her best to forget Clay and put all her hopes for the future, for a real family, into her marriage.

"A lot of women keep their maiden names when they marry," Siobhan said. "Mom was a McKenna all her life because my father died before they could marry. Jeff understood I wanted to keep the family name to honor her."

"Whatever. I really don't care anymore."

"But obviously you do," Siobhan argued. "Why? Because Jeff left the ranch to his wife instead of to his sister?"

Jacy laughed. "You don't understand. You never got it. The reason Jeff didn't leave it to me was because I'm *not* a real Atkinson. I *wasn't* Jeff's sister."

Siobhan started. "What are you talking about?"

"My mother was pregnant when Jeff's father married her. Pregnant by another man. His father let me use the name, but he never formally adopted me. He treated me like I didn't exist. Jeff and I weren't related at all, but two *siblings* were never closer. And I do mean close, Siobhan. *Intimately* so. All those things you didn't really want to do with him? I gladly did them all. I made up for what you wouldn't give him."

Realizing Jacy meant sexual things, Siobhan whispered, "I don't believe you."

Jacy strutted closer, her true nastiness unfettered by good manners or subterfuge. "We'd been doing those things since we were teenagers. You don't think we stopped just because he married you, did you? Why do you think he agreed to marry a woman in love with another man? Because he was so crazy about you?" She shook her head. "You were our cover, Siobhan. Who would think to take a close look at us when he was a happily married man?"

Unable to take this in, to believe that she'd been that big a fool, Siobhan shook her head. "Jeff loved me. I know he did."

"Eventually. You made him fall for you, then everything changed for me. Then he *wanted* to stop sleeping with me, wanted me to find a man who would take me away from the ranch. I was still too much temptation for him. He wanted you to love him the way I did. Jeff tried replacing me, Siobhan, but he couldn't...he kept coming back to me, even when he said he didn't want to. He was angry with himself, the reason he did what he did with the will."

FROM THE SHADOWS OF THE barn, Clay heard it all. He'd tried calling Siobhan, but without her having a cell phone, getting her in person had been impossible. So he'd come back to the ranch to update her in person, to tell her about Buck's murder and Vargas being in a jail cell. About his conclusion that they'd let go of Early Farnum as a suspect too soon. But then, having parked near the house, he'd entered the barn unnoticed and had heard Jacy's confession about her relationship with her supposed brother.

She was still on the attack. "Jeff actually believed you were going to have his children, Siobhan. That's how he justified cheating me of this place."

Clay looked around at the horses. Animals had a sense about people, and all three of them were staying as far away from Jacy as they could. Chief had turned his back on her. Garnet was watching her warily. But Warrior...even from a distance, Clay sensed his enmity.

"Blame your stepfather, then," Siobhan was saying. "He left the spread to Jeff, and it was only natural that Jeff would leave it to his own family."

"What a joke. You hate this place, the ranch that has always been my home!" Jacy snapped. "You had no right to steal it from me! You had no right to steal *Jeff* from me!"

And it suddenly became clear to Clay. "Is that why you killed Jeff?" he asked, stepping out of the shadows. "You killed him out of spite?"

He linked gazes and more with Siobhan to make certain she was all right. She was vulnerable, but she was strong. He could feel the river of fury flowing beneath her controlled exterior.

"Jeff interfered with my plans," Jacy said. "He had Siobhan and the ranch, and I wanted something of my own."

"Uranium?" Clay guessed.

"That would have given me the money I needed to start over."

"Alone? Or with Buck Hale?" Clay asked. "Where did Buck fit in before you killed him, too?"

"Buck's dead?" Siobhan gasped.

Clay nodded. "I found him. Killed with his own kitchen knife."

Jacy reached into her shoulder bag. "I have something

more effective for you." She pulled out a gun which she aimed at Clay.

"Jacy!" Siobhan cried. "Don't!"

Concentrating, Clay opened his mind to Siobhan. *Take it easy. Keep her talking.*

Siobhan's eyes widened, so apparently she "heard" him.

What are you going to do?

Jacy was saying, "I did what I had to do, just as I've always been forced to!"

Warrior snorted and Clay tuned in to the horse. The raised voices were upsetting him. *Jacy* in particular was upsetting him.

"Buck told me there might be uranium deposits on the land," Jacy continued. "I tried to get Jeff interested, but he wouldn't listen to me. He stopped listening to me when he married *you.*"

"So you did it all?" Siobhan asked. "Everything that went wrong on the ranch was due to you?"

Clay edged closer as Jacy kept talking.

"Starting with the bank note being called in. I thought that would convince Jeff we needed to mine the uranium," Jacy said. "But he wouldn't hear of it, so I had to go looking on my own. Well, not exactly on my own. But when I was out there with Buck, trying to find a sample, Jeff stumbled onto us. He was furious, wanted nothing to do with something that would poison the earth, poison good people. He had to be stopped." She shrugged. "Then Buck got out of hand and had to be stopped. Now you two have to be stopped."

Keep her talking, Clay urged Siobhan as he continued

to inch toward the murderess. Then he connected with Warrior, and through thoughts and images urged him to make a ruckus.

"You already tried to kill us," Siobhan said. "That was you shooting at us, not Buck."

"Buck was…indisposed. So I borrowed that old truck of his and came after you."

Warrior squealed and broke to his right, catching Jacy's attention long enough for Clay to act. He lunged at her and got his hands around the gun. She was a big woman and stronger than he'd expected, no doubt from working the ranch. She clung to the gun, so he twisted her arm. Then suddenly there was a blast, and heat searing his side stopped him cold. Flying back, he heard Siobhan scream as he collapsed.

In the distance, Warrior squealed again, louder this time.

Jacy laughed, and the sound was maniacal. "I'll make it seem like Clay murdered Jeff so he could win back the woman he loved. When he couldn't do it, he decided the only way out was a murder-suicide."

Fighting losing consciousness, Clay picked up on Siobhan's thoughts.

I won't let this happen! Hang on, Clay, and I won't let the legacy win this time!

COLD ANGER FILLED SIOBHAN. While Jacy was smirking at Clay on the ground, Siobhan attacked, leading with her shoulder to knock Jacy off balance. When the other woman swung her gun hand around, Siobhan kneed her in the stomach as hard as she could. Jacy doubled over, and Siobhan flew into her again. This time, the gun went spinning out of Jacy's hand, right through the fence boards, landing outside the corral, and Siobhan was on her.

Literally.

They fell to the ground, Siobhan on top, hitting Jacy over and over. Jacy was bigger and stronger and easily flipped her onto her back. She slid her hands around Siobhan's neck and started squeezing.

Warrior was screaming now and Siobhan got a glimpse of him lurching back and forth, as if he was working himself into a fury. Fury aimed at Jacy. Even with the breath being choked out of her, Siobhan was aware of images the horse saw and was buying into, images that could only be coming from Clay.

Unable to take a breath, seeing pinpoints of light behind her eyes, Siobhan picked up on those images and doubled the effort, urging the horse to do something to stop Jacy.

Warrior screamed again and his hooves exploded over the ground as he charged.

Jacy's hands loosened on Siobhan's neck and she glanced back toward the thundering horse. Panicking, she flew up to her feet and tried to run to the gate, but she couldn't outrun a horse. He hit her hard and she went flying, headfirst, into the top fence board.

She collapsed without uttering a sound.

Warrior made one sweep of the pasture and as he passed Jacy's crumpled body, he bucked and kicked her with both hooves as if for good measure.

Gasping for breath, Siobhan crawled to Clay, who

was trying to sit up and not doing a very good job of it. Calmer now, Warrior stopped near them and stood over them protectively as Siobhan gathered Clay in her shaking arms. The front of his T-shirt was wet with his blood. She was grateful she couldn't see red against the black cloth, or she might throw up.

"You're going to live, you hear me!" she ordered Clay. "You can't die. You have to fight until help comes." And then she had to ask, "Where's your cell phone?"

JACY WAS DEAD, HER NECK broken from the fall, her leg broken from where Warrior kicked her. She was already out of sight, camouflaged by a body bag. Siobhan didn't miss the irony of Jacy's fate. She'd somehow made sure that Jeff's neck had been broken. And then his horse's leg. Clay hadn't put that thought into Warrior's mind and neither had she...but there it was.

"It's not his fault," Siobhan told Sheriff Tannen as the medics got Clay's stretcher into the ambulance. "Jacy was crazed. Warrior's still not well from the poisoning," she added, "and he got real upset with all the yelling and the gun going off and Jacy trying to strangle me. He didn't mean to kill her."

Having heard the story from start to finish while waiting for the EMT to arrive, Tannen gave her a puzzled look. "No reason for me to think your horse purposely killed anyone, not even someone as black-hearted as that witch. In my book, Jacy Atkinson caused her own death. I'm sure the district attorney will agree and won't be pressing charges against Warrior there."

Jacy glanced back at the corral. Warrior's head hung

over the top rung as he watched her. She sensed no regret in the horse. He seemed peaceful as he nickered softly then moved away to join Garnet and Chief on the other side of the corral.

Tannen patted her shoulder comfortingly. "Maybe you better get up in that ambulance before they take your man away without you."

"Thanks."

"I'll meet you at the hospital."

She still could hardly believe that her sister-in-law was a murderess, that she'd killed the man who everyone thought was her brother. And Buck Hale, of course. Plus, all the other things that Jacy had done to destroy the ranch…it was simply inconceivable. Had she really thought she would get away with it? Maybe Jacy would have, if not for Clay.

And Jeff's part of it all was inconceivable, as well. After Jacy's confession about their lurid affair, she would never be able to think of her late husband in the same way again.

"Hey," Clay said, finding her hand. "What are you thinking about?"

"That we beat the prophecy," she said, never happier than when she added, "They say you're going to live."

"You, too."

She clasped his hand harder and focused her mind until she connected with him. *I know what you did.*

Got shot.

You showed Warrior what to do. How?

The Irish aren't the only ones who know how to

manipulate the psychic universe. You could learn a thing or two from my grandfather.

She felt Clay drift off then, and she figured whatever they gave him for pain was working.

WHEN CLAY WOKE UP, HE was feeling no pain. Except when he looked at the beautiful mess asleep in the chair next to his hospital bed. Siobhan was dirtier than he'd ever seen her. Her hair was in tangles, though it looked as if she'd finger-combed it. She'd tried to wash up, but her face was streaked rather than clean.

Or were those streaks on her cheeks caused by tears for him?

He loved her more than anything, and because he loved her, he would give her what she wanted. So when her eyes fluttered open and met his and he heard her quick intake of breath preceding her radiant smile, he knew what he had to do.

"I'll be gone at sunrise," he told her.

She swallowed hard and blinked at him. "You're not going anywhere. In case you don't remember, you were shot."

"I feel fine."

She indicated his intravenous line. "Wait till they take away your morphine. You won't be so cocky then."

"Then I'll leave the next day. Or the one after that."

Her expression sobered. "Reconsider."

"Why?"

"I still need you," she admitted in a small voice.

"Don't worry, I'll help you find someone who can run the spread better than I can."

"But he won't *be* you."

"What are you saying?"

"That I love you and I just wanted to protect you from the family curse but…if you were willing to chance it, I was wrong to turn you away."

"Which time?"

"It didn't work the second time." Now she was sounding testy. "You wouldn't go. That took a lot of nerve. Something I lacked. But not anymore. We beat the prophecy, Clay. It's done now. And if it comes back at us, we'll beat it again."

Words he'd waited years to hear. And yet he needed to know more. "You married another man, Siobhan. How do I deal with that? Forget what he was to Jacy, what was he to you?"

"I married Jeff because I cared about him, and because he accepted my feelings for you. I didn't know about him and Jacy. I didn't want to live my life alone like Mom has all these years. I had dreams of a family…" She sighed. "All my planning didn't stop the prophecy from taking Jeff. For that, I will always regret marrying him. He was a good man, Clay, despite a warped relationship with Jacy or not. I still believe that. He was kind to me, generous with his workers, concerned for the environment. One bad thing doesn't change who a person is at heart. It makes them human."

Clay guessed he could understand Siobhan's thinking. He would have to. She was finally willing to give them another chance, and he wasn't about to throw away what was probably his last opportunity to have what he wanted.

Still...

"If I do stay, I have conditions."

"Which are?"

"You get rid of the cow-calf operation and follow your dream of breeding and training horses. I'll help you, but I plan to keep my job at the correctional center."

Her smile lit up her dirty face. "I wouldn't have it any other way."

"One of us needs to make decent money until we know if this thing will work out."

"Besides, you love helping to change lives for the better," Siobhan said, understanding perfectly. "And I have no doubts we're going to work out. We've never stopped loving each other, no matter the circumstances. That's never going to change."

"And if you agree to marry me, will you change your name for me?"

Her grin got wider. "Siobhan McKenna-Salazar. I like it."

And he loved her. He pulled her against him. "Then kiss me like you mean it."

"Gladly," she whispered, as she leaned in to do just that.

* * * * *

⬣ Harlequin

INTRIGUE

COMING NEXT MONTH

Available March 8, 2011

#1263 RANSOM FOR A PRINCE
Cowboys Royale
Lisa Childs

#1264 AK-COWBOY
Sons of Troy Ledger
Joanna Wayne

#1265 THE SECRET OF CYPRIERE BAYOU
Shivers
Jana DeLeon

#1266 PROTECTING PLAIN JANE
The Precinct: SWAT
Julie Miller

#1267 NAVY SEAL SECURITY
Brothers in Arms
Carol Ericson

#1268 CIRCUMSTANTIAL MARRIAGE
Thriller
Kerry Connor

HICNM0211

USA TODAY *bestselling author Lynne Graham*
is back with a thrilling new trilogy
SECRETLY PREGNANT, CONVENIENTLY WED

Three heroines must marry alpha males to keep
their dreams...but Alejandro, Angelo and Cesario
are not about to be tamed!

Book 1—JEMIMA'S SECRET
Available March 2011 from Harlequin Presents®.

JEMIMA yanked open a drawer in the sideboard to find
Alfie's birth certificate. Her son was her husband's child.
It was a question of telling the truth whether she liked it or
not. She extended the certificate to Alejandro.

"This has to be nonsense," Alejandro asserted.

"Well, if you can find some other way of explaining how
I managed to give birth by that date and Alfie not be yours,
I'd like to hear it," Jemima challenged.

Alejandro glanced up, golden eyes bright as blades and
as dangerous. "All this proves is that you must still have
been pregnant when you walked out on our marriage. It
does not automatically follow that the child is mine."

"'I know it doesn't suit you to hear this news now and I
really didn't want to tell you. But I can't lie to you about it.
Someday Alfie may want to look you up and get acquainted."

"If what you have just told me is the truth, if that little
boy does prove to be mine, it was vindictive and extremely
selfish of you to leave me in ignorance!"

Jemima paled. "When I left you, I had no idea that I was
still pregnant."

"Two years is a long period of time, yet you made no
attempt to inform me that I might be a father. I will want
DNA tests to confirm your claim before I make any deci-

sion about what I want to do."

"Do as you like," she told him curtly. "*I* know who Alfie's father is and there has never been any doubt of his identity."

"I will make arrangements for the tests to be carried out and I will see you again when the result is available," Alejandro drawled with lashings of dark Spanish masculine reserve.

"I'll contact a solicitor and start the divorce," Jemima proffered in turn.

Alejandro's eyes narrowed in a piercing scrutiny that made her uncomfortable. "It would be foolish to do anything before we have that DNA result."

"I disagree," Jemima flashed back. "I should have applied for a divorce the minute I left you!"

Alejandro quirked an ebony brow. "And why didn't you?"

Jemima dealt him a fulminating glance but said nothing, merely moving past him to open her front door in a blunt invitation for him to leave.

"I'll be in touch," he delivered on the doorstep.

What is Alejandro's next move? Perhaps rekindling their marriage is the only solution! But will Jemima agree?

Find out in Lynne Graham's
exciting new romance
JEMIMA'S SECRET

Available March 2011
from Harlequin Presents®.

Start your Best Body today with these top 3 nutrition tips!

1. **SHOP THE PERIMETER OF THE GROCERY STORE:** The good stuff—fruits, veggies, lean proteins and dairy—always line the outer edges of the store. When you veer into the center aisles, you enter the temptation zone, where the unhealthy foods live.

2. **WATCH PORTION SIZES:** Most portion sizes in restaurants are nearly twice the size of a true serving and at home, it's easy to "clean your plate." Use these easy serving guidelines:
   - Protein: the palm of your hand
   - Grains or Fruit: a cup of your hand
   - Veggies: the palm of two open hands

3. **USE THE RAINBOW RULE FOR PRODUCE:** Your produce drawers should be filled with every color of fruits and vegetables. The greater the variety, the more vitamins and other nutrients you add to your diet.

Find these and many more helpful tips in

YOUR BEST BODY NOW
by
TOSCA RENO
WITH STACY BAKER

Bestselling Author of
THE EAT-CLEAN DIET

Available wherever books are sold!